Jackson

vs.

Witchy Wanda:

Making Kid Soup

Jackson

vs.

Witchy Wanda:

Making Kid Soup

Belinda Anderson

Mountain State Press

Charleston, WV

International Standard Book Number:
978-0-941092-69-2

Library of Congress Catalog Number:
2013937389

First Edition
Printed in the USA

Cover art by Jeanne Brenneman
Cover Design by Eric Fritzius (misterherman.com)
Typesetting by Cat Pleska and Eric Fritzius
Editor: Cat Pleska (catpleska.com)

Mountain State Press
2300 MacCorkle Ave. S.E.
Charleston, WV 25304
www.mountainstatepress.org

Visit the author at
http://belindaanderson.com

MOUNTAIN
S T A T E
P R E S S

Dedication

Dedicated to you, reader,

because your imagination is the magic that makes books come alive.

Previous books by Belinda Anderson

The Well Ain't Dry, Yet

The Bingo Cheaters

Buckle Up, Buttercup

MOUNTAIN
STATE
PRESS

Contents

A Warning

The wind and the huge gray cloud tried to warn the town. First they swept over a boy at the railroad depot. He looked up at the darkening sky and shivered, even though it was a warm October afternoon.

Cloud's shadow covered the train depot, dimming the usually cheery pumpkin-orange building with its frosting-white trim. Wind pushed the cloud across the street, just as an officer emerged from the police station. He whipped the sunglasses off his broad face, frowned at the sky and retreated back inside.

Glasglen, nestled in a mountain valley, was the kind of town that prided itself on its smallness. It did not take long for the cloud and the wind to travel down Railroad Avenue, past the barbershop, post office, fire station, pharmacy and bank. They turned the corner onto Wickham Street, moving past city hall. Upon reaching the big stone church, founded in 1777, they hesitated, turned and crossed the street, traveling back the way they had come.

Cloud lingered to lengthen the shadows of the granite gravestones propped against one wall of the funeral home. Wind lashed at the monuments. A cat hiding behind one of the tombstones hissed at the cloud and wind, feeling very proud when they moved along to Dewey's Department Store.

Wind paused to swirl before the display window. Inside stood a woman wearing a suit a shade darker than the orange train depot, her eyes a pale blue, her hair flat, one hand on her hip as though she were fed up with everyone and everything. She did not breathe. She did not blink at the miniature tornado of dried brown leaves that the wind commanded to dance before the glass.

Finally perceiving that the woman was a life-sized doll, the wind and cloud continued on to the grocery store, then halted, having arrived once again at the railroad tracks.

Suddenly, the crossing lights began to flash red. A long, loud whistle announced the imminent arrival of a train. The cloud retreated to hover over the gold-and- red wooded hill that lay just behind the grocery and department stores and the funeral home. Sighing, the wind lifted and followed. The town was on its own.

Part One: Making Kid Soup

Jackson McKinney lurked behind the train depot, crouching, trying to lure his prey out of hiding with the chicken tender he'd saved from his school lunch.

He knew his parents would be as steamed as the limp broccoli the school cafeteria had served if they discovered what he was doing. They'd say they couldn't afford to pay for pet food and rabies shots. Then they'd add that he wasn't responsible enough for a pet, even though he was ten. And, anyway, he'd rather have a dog.

But Jackson couldn't stand to watch the little black-and-white cat grow skinnier and skinnier. He'd first seen it darting past the pharmacy when he was walking home from school one day. Another day, he saw it being chased by the fluffy feline that thought it owned the police station. Then he'd spotted the little cat hiding in the shadow of the funeral home, but it had run away when he tried to approach it.

Today, conditions were perfect, though unusual: Even though a train was due soon, there were no passengers hanging around to create a disturbance with their gabbing. The manager, who had just given

Jackson a candy bar, was inside the station, minding his own business.

Jackson peered beneath the station platform. In the gloom, he couldn't see much but two glowing eyes. Gently, Jackson used a single fingertip to push the chicken tender closer.

Just as the little cat had begun to creep forward, head raised, sniffing at the smell of the chicken, the shriek of a whistle sent it running. Jackson sighed and stood, watching the sleek silver train approaching the station. Idly, he rummaged through his pockets. In one lay the candy bar that the station manager had given him. He planned to stash it in his room just in case his mom served zucchini soup again for supper.

In the other pocket rested the lucky penny his grandfather had given him when Grandpa was having one of his good days. The coin was an Indian head penny, with a picture of a Native American wearing a head dress instead of the usual portrait of Abraham Lincoln. "Liberty" paraded in print across the band of the head dress.

Indian head pennies hadn't been minted for nearly a hundred years. Jackson was pretty sure the penny was valuable, because his parents had made a big deal over how special the gift was. He was supposed to keep it on a display stand in his bedroom, but Jackson figured the penny could only bring him luck if he was carrying it. So far, it hadn't helped him catch the cat. Maybe the coin had to be rubbed at the exact moment luck was needed. He'd have to test that theory the next time he saw the cat.

The wind made him wish he'd worn his heavier jacket like his mom had wanted, but it was just the first week in October. Pushed along by the breeze, a flock of fallen orange and yellow leaves scurried across the tracks just as the train arrived.

Jackson stayed by the station platform, curious to see who might be arriving. The train hurtled toward the station so rapidly that Jackson was sure the sleek silver Cardinal would whiz right on by. Then the metal wheels began screeching as they dragged to a halt on the rails, the last car stopping right before Jackson.

Only one passenger came down the steps, making a bumpity-bumpity-bump racket with her big black bag. The woman was beautiful, in a terrible way, tall, with lots and lots of wavy red hair and eyes so dark they swallowed the afternoon sunlight.

She caught Jackson staring at her. "My name," she said, in a voice like slow-running molasses, "is Witchy Wanda, and I have come to add some interest to this town."

Some instinct told him that really she had come to add trouble to the town. But maybe she was just an actress or some kind of celebrity. She could be somebody really famous and he wouldn't know, because his parents disapproved of television and only let him watch a few shows.

"Cat got your tongue, boy?"

Jackson tried to talk, but found himself wondering about her black coat, a robe really, and how it seemed to absorb light. She slipped her hand inside one of the pockets and withdrew a small glass vial.

5

Removing the stopper, she dabbed a bit of liquid on her wrists. "Essence of lily," she said, now smelling so sweet Jackson thought he might suffocate. "Do you think I need more?"

He swallowed and croaked, "No, ma'am."

"Why are you standing there with your hand over your ear?"

Sometimes, when Jackson was nervous, he cradled his hand around his right ear, even though his hearing aid couldn't fall out when he was just standing or sitting. He continued to stare.

"Oh, the silent type. My favorite. Never mind, I'm sure you can point." She was beautiful, all right, but Jackson wasn't sure he liked her. "Come along and show me the way to 42 Crab Apple Street."

Jackson swallowed again, hard. That was his street.

"Step lively. My granny was slow, and you see what happened to her."

Jackson started walking, even though she was a stranger, and he shouldn't even be talking to her. "What happened?"

"She got caught and thrown in the lake." Witchy Wanda walked fast, dragging the big black bag, which continued to make that awful bumpity-bumpity-bump sound. Jackson wondered what could make such a racket. "Pity, really. Just a day short of her 150th birthday."

That was when Jackson figured she was just making stuff up because he was a kid. What she didn't know was that he was a really smart kid. Most of the kids in his fifth-grade class didn't know it, either, because he kept to himself. He read a lot, partly because of the TV deal, but mostly because you never knew when a piece of knowledge might come in handy. He knew, for instance, how to start a fire with a cola can, a bar of chocolate and a thin piece of bark. At least in theory.

"What's your question?"

Startled, Jackson said, "How did you know I had a question?"

"Knitted eyebrows, frown. So?"

"I was just wondering, is Wanda your last name, or is the whole thing a nickname?" For some reason, he didn't want to say the word "Witchy." He didn't want to look too long into those dark eyes, either.

"My name is Witchy Wanda. That's all you need to know."

His mind resisted allowing that name to make a nest in his brain. Instead, he'd think of her as Double W.

She walked along, head turning this way and that, dragging her noisy bag along. "What a charming town."

Maybe. It had a bunch of historic buildings made from historic limestone and historic brick. It had lots of brick: red brick, burgundy brick, brown brick and brick painted in all sorts of colors, from beige to blue. But no cell phone service or wireless computing, which would interfere with the nearby federal observatory's telescope tracking of radio signals in space.

Glasglen didn't even have a skateboard park. Not that Jackson would be allowed to go there, if such a place existed, because he wasn't even allowed to have a skateboard. No way was Jackson going to crack his skull falling off one of those contraptions, his mom had said. When Jackson had argued that he could wear a helmet, his dad said one spill and that'd be the end of the hearing aid, and Jackson ought to know that money didn't grow on trees.

Glasglen's primary attractions were the historic Amtrak station, the coffee shop and Dewey's Department Store, which featured a window-front mannequin that everyone called Miss Margot. She always wore a burnt orange suit that his mom said might have been in style about twenty years ago.

They turned on to Crab Apple Street, the bag following with its bumpity-bumpity-bump racket. He walked right on by his house. Something told him he didn't want her knowing where he lived.

But she slowed her pace. "Cute," she said. "Like a gingerbread cottage." Jackson worried that maybe she'd knock on the door and introduce herself to his parents as a new neighbor, but she resumed her stride. "One of my aunts lived in a gingerbread cottage."

"Did she move?" Jackson asked, hoping to divert her attention.

"Off this mortal coil, yes. Faulty oven."

Jackson wondered what a mortal coil was. Jackson started looking closely at the house numbers, but he suspected he already knew that Witchy Wanda's residence would be the old house across the street. He stopped there, waiting for her to walk through the fence gate barely hanging on its hinges. The wind made the window shutters bang with angry slaps. The house sported a turret that looked like the perfect place to keep someone imprisoned. Jackson and his buddies were under strict orders from their parents to stay away from the place. They would have been tempted to ignore the ban, except for

Jackson's dad mentioning that the overgrown grass would make excellent napping nests for poisonous snakes.

"Surely you don't think I would dwell in a dump like that," his companion said in a voice as cold as a snowball. "Lay on, Macduff."

He guessed that meant he was supposed to keep going. "My name is Jackson," he said, then wished he hadn't told her. "Are you sure this isn't the house?"

"Do you see a 42, Mr. President?" He knew she was making a joke about his name, but he didn't think it was particularly funny. "I don't see a 42."

"Jackson is my first name," he informed her. "My last name is McKinney." Then he wished he hadn't told her that, either.

"McKinney, hmm? Could be Scottish, could be Irish."

"I'm American," Jackson said.

"Blond hair, blue eyes," she said, ignoring his statement. "Probably Scottish. Very tender skin." The black bag dragging behind her with its mysterious cargo bumpity-bumped in agreement.

They continued to walk. "Ah, here we are," Witchy Wanda said.

They stopped in front of a spectacular contemporary home. Eyesore, his father called it, saying at least the old wreck across the street once had some sense of style. Most houses took the shape of a rectangle or square. This one looked sort of like a trapezoid with its crazy angles.

Witchy Wanda reached into the pocket of her robe coat and withdrew a key.

9

"See you," Jackson said, ready to run.

"What's your hurry?" She opened the door. "I could use some help," she said, though she dragged the bag inside all by herself.

No way Jackson was going inside a stranger's house. Just then a hand seized his shoulder and pulled him through the door.

Jackson found himself standing inside a big empty room with a huge fireplace, polished wooden floors and a ceiling as high as a church. "I'm supposed to go home straight after school."

"That train has already left the station, hasn't it?" Witchy Wanda said, laughing at the joke that Jackson didn't think was very funny. "It's a little chilly in here. I think I'll start a fire. Oh, good, the departed occupants left some wood." As she bent at the fireplace, her robe billowed and Jackson couldn't see exactly what she was doing. When she straightened, flames roared. Jackson wanted to ask if the departed occupants had left kindling and a box of matches, too, but he remained silent.

"Now, you could at least help me unpack my things," she said. "Didn't your parents teach you to be helpful to older people?"

Witchy Wanda did not belong in the category of older people in Jackson's opinion, but he followed her as she dragged her bag through the great room and into the kitchen. He'd help her and then he'd scoot home.

Jackson couldn't believe it when she opened the bag and brought forth a copper kettle big enough to poach a goat. Next, she scooped a bunch of bottles and jars from the suitcase and set them on the counter. Finally, she brought out a bundle wrapped in a red cloth. She placed the bundle on the counter and unrolled it to reveal chopping knives, a ladle and some other utensils. "You could sort the spices for me."

"That's it?" Jackson asked. "That's all you brought? Cooking stuff?"

"Just the essentials." She bent and opened a cabinet. "I often find the departed occupants leave useful items. Like this." She held up a pitcher, which she took to the sink and filled. She dumped the water in the kettle, then another pitcher full and then another and yet another. Finally, she picked up the pot. She must be really strong.

Jackson followed her to the great room, where she settled the kettle in the fireplace. "There's nothing like homemade soup," Witchy Wanda said.

"You're going to make soup here?" Jackson asked. "You've got a microwave oven in the kitchen. And a regular stove."

"I am indeed going to make soup right here. And you're going to help me."

"I'm going home," he said.

11

Witchy Wanda seemed to grow taller. She held one arm straight out and pointed a finger at him. "Jackson McKinney," she said in a deep, deep voice. "I cast a spell on you."

She was a real witch! Jackson closed his eyes, expecting to be scorched by a lightning bolt or something even worse. When nothing happened, he opened his eyes. Witchy Wanda looked surprised, too.

"Jackson McKinney," she repeated, her voice dropping even lower, "I cast a spell on you."

"Umm, aren't you supposed to use words with lots of syllables when you cast spells?" She wasn't a real witch, after all. She was just trying to kid with him.

Witchy Wanda didn't look like she was kidding, though. "You're a little young to have a heart pacemaker," she said. She walked around him as though trying to figure out what species he might be. She said, "What have we here?"

Not quite catching her words, Jackson said, "What about my ear?" As soon as he spoke, Jackson knew he had given himself away.

Witchy Wanda bent and squinted into his right ear. "That's a problem."

"What's a problem?"

Witchy Wanda considered him. "Since it won't matter in five minutes, I'll tell you. Spells can't be cast on subjects with electronic devices that interact with their bodies. Disrupts the energy flow of the spell."

He wondered why she just didn't yank the aid from his ear. Then he figured it out. She couldn't touch it directly. That's why she wouldn't use the microwave.

"What difference does five minutes make?"

Witchy Wanda smiled at him. She was extremely beautiful when she smiled. "Because in five minutes, you're going to be boiled, Jackson. I don't need a spell to pick up a shrimp like you."

Before Jackson knew what was happening, Witchy Wanda grabbed him and threw him into the hot kettle of water.

Jackson coughed and sputtered, but Wanda slammed the lid on the kettle and snapped it closed. "Locking lids," she said. "What a wonderful innovation in cookery."

The water stopped just short of Jackson's nose and ears. But it was becoming very hot, especially in the seat of his pants. He heard his captor's footsteps heading for the kitchen. Before he could formulate a plan of escape, she returned, singing,

Witchy Wanda, Witchy Wanda,
Making Soup, Making Soup

She unsnapped the lid and flung black powder in his face. Jackson started to leap from the pot, but sneezed instead, and she quickly slammed the lid again and locked it once more. The pepper stung Jackson's eyes. His legs felt like they were sunburned.

Just then the doorbell rang. "Most inconvenient," Witchy Wanda said. Jackson heard her open the door.

"Excuse me, ma'am." Jackson recognized the voice even before it said, "I'm Officer Kearns."

"Oh, Officer, come in," the villain said in that sweet molasses voice, and Jackson knew exactly why. Officer Kearns would make a very chunky stew. Officer Kearns made up in width for what he was missing in height, though he could chase Jackson and his buddies away from interesting Dumpsters. And Jackson could never figure out how such a solid mass could sneak up on turkey and deer, but he had a reputation as a skilled hunter.

"Ma'am, I'm looking for a little boy. His parents say he's gone missing."

"What a shame," Witchy Wanda said. "Have you tried looking at the railroad station? Little boys love trains."

Jackson tried to yell, but succeeded only in gurgling soup water. He banged on the side of the kettle with his fists, but they made no sound. Struggling to reach inside his pocket, he fished out the penny and struck it against the cauldron again and again.

"What the–" he heard Officer Kearns say. It sounded like he was walking toward the pot.

14

"Officer Kearns, I cast a spell on you."

As soon as Witchy Wanda spoke those words, Jackson knew he would have to rescue himself. He began rocking back and forth, back and forth, until finally he gained enough momentum to knock the kettle over. The lid snapped open and Jackson and the water spilled out. The water flowed right over Witchy Wanda's sharp-toed black boots.

"I'm melting, I'm melting!" Witchy Wanda shrieked. But she remained unpuddled. "Just kidding."

Officer Kearns laughed as though Witchy Wanda was the most clever woman he had ever met. "Good one," he said. "That's from an old movie or something, right?" The officer frowned at Jackson. "What are you doing, bothering this nice lady? Your folks are worried sick about you."

Jackson figured standing around and arguing would just give Witchy Wanda another chance to stuff him back in the pot. He stood and shot out the door, running as fast as he could. The sun would be setting soon, and he'd be glad to be home by dark. He had almost made it to his house when he stopped. Witchy Wanda had not pursued him. That could mean only one thing. Next on the menu: Officer Kearns.

So what? A police officer could look after himself, even if he was under a witch's spell. He had a gun, after all. But a gun might not even put a dent in something as tough as a witch. Still, why should Jackson worry about Officer Kearns, who didn't even like kids? Then

Jackson remembered the time Officer Kearns had found Jackson's grandfather, who had some kind of disease that made him confused sometimes and wanting to wander.

Officer Kearns had spotted Jackson's grandfather walking along a highway, determined to find a recruitment office where he could enlist to go fight the enemy. Officer Kearns gave him a ride, telling him he was awfully brave. By the time they got back to the McKinneys' house, Grandpa had forgotten all about war. Now, Grandpa couldn't go very far because he needed a walker, but Jackson remembered how awful he had felt when he thought Grandpa was gone forever.

Reluctantly, Jackson turned around and started back for 42 Crab Apple. No use trying to get any adults to help – they'd tell him there was no such thing as a witch. And even if he had time to find his classmates, they'd tell him he was nuts. If something was going to be done, Jackson would have to do it.

Witchy Wanda, Witchy Wanda
Making Soup, Making Soup

Cold and wet, Jackson crept in the twilight around the shrubbery and through the weedy flowers around Witchy Wanda's house. Seeds flew out from the white heads of the stalky Queen Anne's Lace, clinging to his clothes. His mom would have a fit, but that couldn't be helped.

16

Jackson followed the sound of the singing, which sounded as though it was coming from a deep male voice. Every time he stepped on a bird's nest-shaped blossom, more seeds attacked his clothing. Grandpa once told Jackson that farmers called the flower Devil's Plague because cows' milk would taste bitter after they ate it. You could eat the roots, because Queen Anne's Lace was the same thing as a wild carrot, but his grandfather said better not because it looked a lot like poison hemlock.

Finding a window, Jackson peeked inside the house. He saw Officer Kearns pouring a pitcher of water into the kettle. "Is that enough?" he asked. Then he climbed into the pot, smiling.

Craning his neck left and right, Jackson could see no sign of Witchy Wanda. Probably in the kitchen, gathering her spices. Jackson eased the window open and called softly, "Officer."

Officer Kearns turned his head and smiled. Then he sang,

Witchy Wanda, Witchy Wanda
Making Soup, Making Soup

"Shhh! Come on." Jackson tried to wave Officer Kearns toward the window.

Officer Kearns started splashing the water on himself. "Wish I had my ducky," he said.

"Shhh! She'll hear you." Jackson waved frantically.

"Who?" Officer Kearns continued to splash.

17

"You know," Jackson said. He didn't want to say her name. "Double W. Get out while you can." A newly formed breeze chilled him through his wet clothes.

Suddenly he smelled the super sweet scent of lily. "Excellent advice," said a sweet female voice. "Too bad you didn't take it yourself."

Before Jackson could turn around, he'd been shoved through the window and back into the house. Witchy Wanda climbed through the window after him and tossed him in the copper cauldron.

"Whee!" said Officer Kearns, whose face was turning very rosy.

At first, the hot water actually felt good, but Jackson began trying to scramble out. "Officer," Witchy Wanda said, "Would you be so kind as to incapacitate your companion?"

Officer Kearns grinned and grabbed Jackson in a bear hug. Trying to wriggle free, Jackson found himself in an even tighter grip. Jackson almost passed out from the cloud of steam attacking him with the smell of the officer's sweat and his garlic breath. The water was so hot it felt like a billion bees were stinging him.

Witchy Wanda bore down on them with the lid, then paused. She fished in the pocket of her robe and drew out a ladle. "Always wise to check the seasoning," she said.

Witchy Wanda dipped the spoon into the pot and scooped a generous amount of soup water. She swallowed it all, and said, "Hmm, needs more–" Suddenly, she stuck her tongue out. "Carrot!" Her eyes bulged and her ears turned red. "Devil's plague!"

18

She started flickering, and then she began shrinking until nothing was left but a shiny black stone shaped like a heart. Not a Valentine, but a real heart. Awesome. Truly.

Officer Kearns slumped and Jackson broke free of his hold to clamber out of the kettle. He raced over to the stone that a minute before had been Witchy Wanda and kicked it with his dripping shoe. Nothing. He bent and touched it. Cold. The witch was toast. Jackson stuck the stone in his pocket.

What had made her turn to stone? It must have been something in the soup. Maybe what he thought was Queen Anne's Lace had really been poison hemlock, and whatever stuck to his clothes had dissolved into the soup.

Officer Kearns moaned and stepped out of the cauldron. He stretched, then gazed about, like he was waking up. He looked down at his sopping clothes, then at Jackson. "I don't know what's going on here," he said. "But you're in a world of trouble."

Jackson figured the worst part of the day was having to stand at the door of his home and listen to his parents praise and thank Officer Kearns for returning their beloved child to them unharmed.

But the day got worse after Officer Kearns left and Jackson found himself grounded without television privileges, meager as they were.

Worse, he discovered his parents were going to volunteer his services at Dewey's Department Store after school until he'd finished his punishment.

Jackson wanted to stomp away, but figured that'd just earn him more prison time, so he walked silently to his room to change out of his wet clothes and into his pajamas. He pulled the stone out of his pocket and set it on his dresser, beside the now soggy candy bar that his parents didn't know the train station manager had given him. Maybe it'd dry out.

Tomorrow, he promised himself, he'd let Amtrak crush Double W. Like every kid in Glasglen, he'd been warned not to play on the railroad tracks, and he wasn't going to. He did not want to end up like the station manager with nothing in his left sleeve. The manager had lost that arm as a teen stepping between what he thought were stopped freight cars. All it had taken was one small lurch forward to change his life forever. Jackson would check the schedule and deposit Double W on the track well before the train's scheduled arrival. He'd do it right after the last class, before he had to report to Dewey's.

Removing his hearing aid from his ear, and the battery from the aid, Jackson placed the device in an electronic box also sitting on the dresser. His parents had explained to him that the box used infrared technology to keep the hearing aid dry. Sometimes Jackson liked to pretend that the special box made him a superhero. Tonight, though, he just felt tired. He turned out the light and climbed into bed. Exhausted, he fell asleep immediately.

20

Jackson did not see a small sliver of moonlight snaking its way through a crack in the curtains. The moonbeam shone on the stone, which began to glow, despite its blackness.

Jackson tossed and turned in his sleep, disturbed by images of Witchy Wanda. One particular scary memory of her slamming the lid on him awakened him. "Just a dream," he muttered. He closed his eyes, but couldn't go back to sleep. He opened his eyes again. Maybe it was the moonlight that was bothering him.

Before he could rise from his bed to close the curtains, he noticed a glow from his dresser. As he stared, the stone began to vibrate until it exploded into a cloud of sparkling, swirling black particles. The bits swirled and formed themselves into the shape of a woman.

The glow faded and Witchy Wanda stood on the floor clutching her head. "I don't feel so good." She looked around and saw Jackson. She stretched a hand toward him. Even without his hearing aid, he was sure she said, "I'll wring your neck and take you home for a nice chowder."

Jackson figured he had to be dreaming, though he could smell lilies.

Witchy Wanda took a step toward him, then faltered. Her legs wobbled and she fell to the floor. "I don't suppose you have any toxic waste on you, do you?" she said, clutching her head again.

"Why do you want toxic paste?" Jackson stared. "You're dead."

"It's true you almost did me in with the carrot trick, but not quite."

"It wasn't carrots, it was poison hemlock." At least he figured it must have been poison hemlock. How could carrots kill a witch?

"Hemlock is delicious," Witchy Wanda said. "I certainly know the difference between dessert and that nasty vegetable."

"You mean the Queen Anne's Lace?" Jackson asked.

"Devil's Plague. Don't ennoble it with a pretty name." Witchy Wanda grabbed the dresser and pulled herself upright. Spying the candy bar, she grabbed it and tore away the wet paper, cramming the confection in her mouth. She chewed quickly and swallowed. "Sweet, sweet chemicals," she said. "Artificial flavorings, dyes, preservatives – I feel better already."

Witchy Wanda spotted the box on the dresser. "What's this? Treasure?" She extended a hand, then drew it back as though she'd been burned.

She tried to approach Jackson, then wobbled again. She changed direction, heading for the door to the hall. "I'll just find myself a broom and be on my way." She turned at the door and pointed to him. "I have not finished my business with you." Then she staggered out the door.

22

What a crazy dream. Jackson closed his eyes. He was so tired. But he was hungry, too. He'd never had any supper. Jackson got up, turned on the light and walked over to his dresser. Instead of the candy bar, he found only a shredded wrapper.

Jackson rubbed his eyes. He didn't see the stone, either. He turned on the overhead light, just to make sure. The rock was gone, all right.

Witchy Wanda could be anywhere, causing all kinds of trouble. Exhausted as he was, Jackson dragged his shoes out from beneath his bed. He started opening the drawers to his dresser, trying to find a flashlight. His heart was racing, and he started to sweat. He was scared of the idea of sneaking out in the night, but he was more scared of what – or whom – Witchy Wanda might be cooking up.

"Jackson, what's all the racket?" It was his father's voice, calling to him from the living room. "Don't make me come in there."

Jackson shut the dresser drawers, kicked his shoes back under the bed, turned out the light and crawled back in bed. If he made his parents any madder, he'd probably never watch TV again until he was in high school.

Witchy Wanda had been pretty weak – maybe it'd take her some time to recover her strength. Maybe she'd just leave town. Maybe …

Jackson's tired body finally won out over his worried mind and he fell asleep.

While Jackson slept, down the road a robed figure stooped over a small body. A sharp-toed black boot prodded the lifeless lump of silvery gray fur.

Witchy Wanda smiled. "Why did the possum cross the road?" she said aloud. "We'll never know, since he didn't make it." She giggled, then picked up the dead animal by the tail. It wouldn't make as nice a soup as a plump policeman or a tender child, but it'd do. For now.

Part Two: Double W's Halloween Party

Jackson woke up to find the sun shining on his face. He stretched and carefully slid out of bed to minimize any effort necessary to make it up to his mother's satisfaction.

He yawned and made his way over to the dresser for his hearing aid. He saw the shredded candy wrapper and he really woke up. Oh, no. Witchy Wanda could be anywhere, just waiting to pounce on him again.

Or maybe not, Jackson tried to persuade himself as he dressed. Maybe she'd left town.

But maybe she hadn't. He had to know. He'd go by her house on the way to school. If he was careful, and stayed out of reach, he'd be OK. His gut told him differently, but Jackson decided it'd be better to confront Witchy Wanda instead of waiting for her to come after him.

He grabbed his back pack and clattered down the stairs. He'd already yanked open the door, determined to get going before his courage could fail him, when his mother called from the kitchen. "Jackson, is that you? Come eat breakfast."

"No time," Jackson hollered. "Got to get to school."

"Don't make me come in there," his father hollered back from the kitchen.

Fifteen minutes later, full of oatmeal and orange juice he hadn't wanted, Jackson was out the door and down the street. In his pocket rode an apple he'd grabbed from the kitchen. If he could somehow trick Witchy Wanda into eating something healthy, maybe she'd turn back into a stone. This time, he wouldn't waste his chance. He'd take her straight to the train tracks.

Jackson stopped when he saw smoke drifting from the chimney of number 42. Uh oh. That had to mean Witchy Wanda was simmering something – or somebody. He couldn't go in. But not knowing would be worse. He had to go in. Jackson walked up to the door and turned the knob ever so slowly, trying to be as quiet as he could.

He pushed the door open just enough to make sure Witchy Wanda wasn't standing there, ready to grab him. He sniffed. No odor of lily at the doorway. Jackson slipped inside and made his way toward the great room, where he heard the sound of off-key singing:

Witchy Wanda, Witchy Wanda,
Making Soup, Making Soup

Witchy Wanda stood with her back to him, stirring something evil-smelling in the big copper kettle in the fireplace. The ladle bumpity-bumped against the kettle as though it were singing along.

Jackson was trying to decide how to hide in a room without furniture when she turned and smiled at him. "Ah, you're just in time for breakfast."

She wasn't rushing toward him, so Jackson stood his ground, trying not to shake. He fingered the apple in his pocket. "I've already had breakfast."

The steam from the kettle curled Witchy Wanda's red hair prettily around her face. "So that's why you stink of whole grain and fresh fruit." She sighed. "I'm tempted to add you as an ingredient, but now you'd just contaminate the broth."

So he was safe for the moment, thanks to the oatmeal and orange juice. "Whatever's in that pot stinks worse." It smelled liked she was stewing something that had been dead for a long time.

"You don't care for possum?" Witchy Wanda reached into the pocket of what looked like the same black robe she wore the day before. Drawing out a pair of enormous silver tongs, she dipped them into the kettle and brought forth a dripping carcass. "Some would argue it's best to remove the hide first, but I prefer the full flavor." She opened the tongs and the possum dropped with a plop back into the kettle.

Jackson thought he was going to lose the oatmeal and orange juice right there on the wooden floor, but the grin on Witchy Wanda's face made him mad enough to ignore his stomach. "I guess you killed that poor animal, just like you tried to kill me."

27

"No, I found him already expired. Wasn't that convenient?" She reached into her other pocket and withdrew a box of pepper. "He needs just a bit more seasoning."

Jackson reached into his own pocket for the apple. He wasn't about to get close enough for her to grab him, though. Instead, he rolled it across the floor to her. "Here. My mom always bakes apples with ham."

Witchy Wanda looked at the apple, a gorgeous red specimen, lying at her feet. "Now, why would you want to do me a favor?" Nonetheless, she picked it up. "It would be a shame to cook something this divine." She took a big bite, not even bothering to wipe off the dust from the floor. "Delicious." She took another bite. Jackson had to stop himself from grinning. Pretty soon she'd start flickering, then shrinking into stone. Next stop, smash-ville.

Instead, her face grew even rosier and prettier. She took yet another bite, and another. She gnawed the apple all the way to its core, and then ate that, too. Not one flicker. She looked at Jackson and laughed. "I'm guessing by the expression on your face that you were anticipating a different reaction." She arranged her own expression into one of mock indignation. "You weren't trying to poison me, were you?"

Jackson's silence provided his answer.

Witchy Wanda laughed again. "Think, Jackson McKinney. You presented me with an apple perfectly shaped, with absolutely no blemishes. Your gift – and I do appreciate it – was loaded with yummy pesticides."

Jackson started backing up. He was out of ammunition and ideas. Witchy Wanda made no attempt to stop him. "Run along to school," she said. "I'll catch you later." She winked. "And I mean that literally."

Jackson ran.

Jackson got into trouble at school for not paying attention. But how could he concentrate on adjectives and equations when there was a homicidal maniac on the loose? He considered his options. He could tell his parents what was happening. He could go to the police station and try talking to Officer Kearns. But Jackson knew Officer Kearns wouldn't remember anything about the time he was under her spell, and no adult would believe that a witch had moved to town.

After school, he headed for the train depot. He knew he had to find a way to defeat Witchy Wanda, but he couldn't let the stray go hungry. As he passed by the police station, the fluffy cat detached itself from its napping spot near the door.

Unlike the scrawny orphan Jackson was trying to help, this cat looked very well fed. Or maybe it just had a lot of fur. It was almost all white, except for a little swath of black under the chin that looked like a beard, and another running in a diagonal over one eye, like a

29

pirate's patch. "This isn't for you," he said, patting his pocket where he'd stowed a bit of cheese wrapped in a napkin. In response, he received a hiss and a swipe at his pants.

At the train station, Jackson didn't see the stray. Probably scared away by a little boy and girl hollering, "Choo choo!" as they boarded the Amtrak train with an older man and woman who must be their grandparents. Clouds blocked the sun, threatening rain. The shiny silver Cardinal began pulling out, scattering red and yellow leaves as it picked up speed. Jackson saw his classmates Rodney and Mumps throwing rocks at the departing train. Idiots. What they were doing was wrong, but what could Jackson do about it? And how come Officer Kearns couldn't show up?

Jackson pulled the cheese out of his pocket, then stuffed it back. No way the cat would emerge with all that noise. His hand absently sought the penny, but it wasn't there. Jackson rummaged in the other pocket. Not there, either. He must have dropped it when he took the wad of cheese and napkin out of his pocket. Panicking, he bent over, looking for the shine of copper in the gravel. He had to find that penny. His parents would kill him if he lost it. Worse, his grandfather would be disappointed in him.

"What're you looking for? Your brains?" Jackson looked up to see Rodney and his sidekick, Mumps. With a nickname like Mumps and a face like a pie crust, the kid was practically forced into becoming a bully. Rodney had just been born mean, Jackson figured.

Rodney was taller than the rest of the kids in the class, with long arms and sharp elbows that Jackson had felt more than once.

Rodney opened his mouth again, but Jackson couldn't hear what he was saying. Was something wrong with his hearing aid? Now both Rodney and Mumps were mouthing words in huge, exaggerated motions. Then he got it. They weren't really saying anything. "What's the matter, you deaf or something?" Rodney asked, this time in a normal voice.

Just ignore them, his mother had advised him about bullies, way back in kindergarten when Jackson had come home crying because he'd been shoved at recess and told to go away, that no one wanted to play with him. Sometimes her advice worked. He suspected that today it wouldn't, but he stayed quiet and dropped his eyes. There lay the penny. He reached for the coin, but Rodney's hand snatched it first.

"Look here, Mumps," he said. "I found a lucky penny."

"That's mine," Jackson said. "My grandfather gave it to me."

"Finders keepers," Rodney said.

"Give it here," Jackson insisted.

"Or what?" Rodney and Mumps both laughed.

Jackson considered. If he grabbed for the penny, he knew Rodney would push him to the ground and he'd probably get beaten up by both Rodney and Mumps. But the penny just might roll loose and maybe he could grab it and get away.

Just as he was about to launch himself toward Rodney, the patrol car of Officer Kearns came creeping by. The car pulled up beside them. Officer Kearns rolled down the window. "You boys look kind of tense. What's up?"

Finally, justice. "He took my penny," Jackson said.

"What penny?" Officer Kearns asked.

"That one." Jackson pointed to Rodney's clenched fist.

"It's my penny," Rodney lied. "Jackson tried to take it from me."

"It's an Indian head penny," Jackson said. "My grandfather gave it to me."

"Tell you what," Officer Kearns said. "Why don't you boys hop in and we'll visit your folks and find out where that penny belongs?"

No way was Jackson going to let his parents know he'd been fooling around with the valuable coin that was supposed to be in his room. And if they saw Officer Kearns one more time, he'd never get to watch television again. "That's OK," he said. "He can keep it." For now, he thought to himself. Rodney grinned.

"Case solved," Officer Kearns said. He looked at Jackson. "Aren't you due somewhere? Thought I heard you were going to be helping Martin Dewey at his store."

"Yes, sir," Jackson said. But he didn't move, waiting for Officer Kearns to pull away. No way was Rodney keeping that penny.

The patrol car didn't move, either. Officer Kearns yanked a thumb. "The store's that direction."

Jackson turned and walked away. Bullies one, Jackson zero.

Jackson trudged along the sidewalk, passing the post office and the pharmacy on his way to Dewey's Department Store. The building was old, old, old, with curlicues decorating the roofline. A fine example of Art Deco architecture, his father had once told him, dating back to the 1930s.

When Jackson had asked if Art Deco was the guy that built the store, his dad had laughed and said that no, Art Deco was a style, like the Goth kids at the high school that dyed their hair black and always wore dark clothes.

Pausing before the display window, Jackson eyed the motionless mannequin. Miss Margot appeared as though she'd been around just as long as the store. Her chin-length brown hair looked lank rather than sleek, and the red on her lips had faded. Her blue eyes had faded, too, giving her a spooky stare. One plastic hand rested on the hip of her burnt orange skirt. The other hovered in the air as though she were about to adjust the lapel on her jacket. Beside her sat a round, brown suitcase that looked like it might have been a crocodile once.

Jackson pushed open the oak door and immediately wrinkled his nose at the strong smell of lemon furniture polish. A little metal bell tinkled his arrival, but Jackson saw no evidence of Mr. Dewey, or any customers, either. No women poking among the racks of modest dresses and blouses. No girls mooning over the jewelry in the big wood-and-glass display cases. No men rummaging among the leather wallets or the navy and black socks. No boys assessing the model trains shelved too high for a kid to reach.

Mr. Dewey emerged from black curtains covering a doorway at the back of the store. A tall, rangy man who wore wire-rimmed glasses, he was mostly bald, except for a fringe of white that looked like icing piped around his ears. He looked about as old as Miss Margot, wearing a suit as black as the curtains.

Jackson remembered his last encounter with Mr. Dewey. Jackson had stepped into the store, looking for a birthday gift for his mother, and picked up a bottle of cologne. Just as he had removed the stopper to take a sniff, a deep voice behind him said, "You break it, you bought it." Startled, Jackson spilled the cologne, spreading the aroma of vanilla through the store. He had to buy the bottle then. He had gone home and filled the half-empty bottle with tap water, hoping his mother wouldn't notice. She'd had to sniff a couple of times to pick up the scent when she opened the present. "Umm, very nice," she'd said. "Delicate. Very delicate."

Mr. Dewey, who smelled somewhat like lemon furniture polish himself, stared briefly at Jackson, then disappeared behind the curtains. He reappeared with a bucket and a squeegee, which he thrust at Jackson. "There you go, young McKinney."

Jackson took the items and awaited further instruction. But Mr. Dewey just stared at him with brown eyes that Jackson thought could be twinkling merrily – or shining scarily. Maybe it was just a trick of the light on Mr. Dewey's glasses.

Finally, Jackson spoke. "What do you want me to do?"

Mr. Dewey extended an aged hand covered with raised purple veins, turned Jackson around and steered him to the front of the store. Mr. Dewey gestured at the interior of the display window. "I'll be in the back. Summon me if a customer needs assistance."

Not much danger of that, Jackson thought as Mr. Dewey departed. This was the time of day when kids were doing homework and the adults were rushing home from work to walk the dog and start supper. Jackson looked at the display platform, half as tall as he. How was he supposed to climb up there with a bucket full of ammonia water?

Jackson set the bucket and squeegee on the platform, then clambered up, nearly knocking over Miss Margot's suitcase as he hoisted himself. When he picked up the bucket, he saw with dismay that it had left a water ring on the wooden surface. He whipped off his t-shirt and tried to rub the stain away, without much success. Maybe it would look all right when it dried. He wriggled back into his shirt and set to work on the window, using the same technique his dad had taught him for cleaning the car windshield at the gas station. Dip the squeegee in the liquid, turn it vertically to drain the excess cleaner, then swipe the glass with the wet foam side of the squeegee. Flip and scrape the glass dry and clean with the rubber blade.

Dip, drain, scrape. The acid smell of the ammonia made him a little dizzy. What was he going to do about Witchy Wanda? Dip, drain, scrape. Where was she now? Dip, drain, scrape.

A tapping at the window interrupted his thoughts. Rodney stood on the other side of the window, pecking on the glass with Jackson's Indian head penny. Jackson slammed the bucket on the platform, determined to race outside to catch the thief and recover his stolen property. Instead, he collided with Miss Margot. As he disentangled himself from the mannequin, he heard loud laughter and saw Rodney and Mumps running away.

"Miscreant."

Jackson nodded his agreement, then realized he hadn't spoken. Had Mr. Dewey heard the ruckus and come to investigate? Jackson peered around the figure of Miss Margot, but saw no sign of the old man.

When he thought about it, the voice was female. Maybe a customer had walked in and he hadn't heard the bell. He looked around the store. Nope.

"Miscreant," the voice repeated.

No doubt about it. Female. And standing right beside him. Awesome. Truly. Before meeting Witchy Wanda, the sudden transformation of a plastic mannequin into a warm body would have sent him screaming into the street. Now, he said, "Yeah, that's Rodney."

"I was referring to you," said Miss Margot. As a real woman, her hair looked soft and shiny. She still looked cool and distant, but she was as beautiful as Witchy Wanda.

"Me? What'd I do?" Jackson asked.

"Let me count the ways," she said, straightening the cuffs of her jacket sleeves with perfectly manicured hands. "First, you most inconsiderately assaulted me. Second, you neglected to apologize. Third, you failed to defend my honor in front of those oafs. Lastly, you've marred my stage with an unsightly stain, which I'm sure you'll try to cover with my suitcase."

Jackson looked at the suitcase, which was just the right size to hide the water stain. Immediately, he seized it and dragged it to the scene of his accidental crime. It was surprisingly heavy. "What's in here?" he asked.

"Open it and find out."

"I better not. Mr. Dewey wouldn't like me snooping."

"That is my suitcase and its contents belong to me."

Suddenly, Jackson became suspicious. "Do you like soup?"

"I despise soup," Miss Margot said.

"Do you like candy bars?"

Miss Margot looked horrified. "Do you think I could maintain a figure like this eating candy bars?"

So maybe she wasn't Witchy Wanda in disguise. "How is it that suddenly you can talk?"

"I don't know," she said and blinked. "I'm feeling rather sleepy. I could do with a nap." And just like that, she was her plastic self again.

"Miss Margot?" Jackson said. "Miss Margot?"

He heard a clanking sound from behind the curtains and a curse. Then Mr. Dewey entered from the back of the store. "Are you calling me, McKinney? What do you want?"

"Uh, I'm finished." Jackson handed Mr. Dewey the bucket and the squeegee and jumped down from the platform. "What do you want me to do now?"

Mr. Dewey looked at the drops of rain starting to splatter the exterior window. "You'd better go on home. Looks like an evil storm brewing. And McKinney–"

"Yes, sir?"

"Don't take it upon yourself to change the display. You leave the mannequin alone, and especially the suitcase. That's my retirement."

Jackson didn't know what he meant, unless the suitcase was a valuable antique, or unless there really was money in there. "Yes, sir." He walked to the door, then turned. "Mr. Dewey?"

"Yes?" Mr. Dewey sounded impatient.

"Let's say, theoretically, that somebody left something wet on a piece of furniture and it left a ring–"

"What? Where?" Mr. Dewey looked wildly about the store. "Did some imbecile set a soda can on one of my cases? A bottled water?"

"No, no," Jackson said. "I was just wondering what you could do about it. It's for a school project," he finished, lamely. Mr. Dewey

38

relaxed a few degrees. "Rub toothpaste over the stain with a clean, damp cloth. Then wipe it dry and polish it." He almost smiled, as though he knew a secret. "Tell your mother it works wonders."

Although it was still mid-afternoon when Jackson left the store, the sky had turned dark. Shrugging his backpack over his shoulders, he ran down the street, trying to beat the rain. When the wind and water began lashing at him, Jackson decided to take refuge at the grocery store until the worst of the storm had passed.

Unburdening himself from the backpack, Jackson settled on the sidewalk under the store awning. He wanted gum, but he was broke. He didn't have even one cent, which reminded him of the Indian head penny. Brooding about how to recover it, he suddenly realized that Miss Margot had come to life right after Rodney had tapped on the window with the lucky penny.

Maybe the penny was magical. Crazy, but no crazier than a talking mannequin or a soupy witch. He had to rescue that penny the next day, even if it meant fighting Rodney, and even if he lost all his teeth in the process.

Just then, a woman with wild red hair and a black robe swept by, trailed by the scent of lily. Leaving a huge black umbrella by the door, she entered the grocery. Witchy Wanda appeared to be going shopping.

Jackson jumped up and followed Witchy Wanda into the grocery, ducking behind other shoppers so she wouldn't see him. He watched her lay a hand on the arm of a teen stacking cans of corn. "Sweets," she said in that sugary molasses voice. "Where do you keep them, young man?"

The young man, pushing back the brown hair flopping over his forehead, gaped at her, then said, "Do you mean candy?"

"Certainly. Show me the candy."

Obediently, the stocker led her to an aisle stocked entirely with Halloween merchandise. Jackson crept along, hiding behind a shopper with a cart – and a broad backside. The shopper stopped to deliberate among the bags of miniature chocolate bars.

Witchy Wanda clapped her hands together like a child who'd just had a wheelbarrow full of presents dumped at her feet. She plucked a bag of candy eyeballs from a shelf. "Aren't these darling!" She ripped open the bag and popped one of the eyeballs in her mouth. "Fantastic," she said. "I don't believe this contains one natural ingredient."

"Ma'am, you can't do that," the stocker protested. "You have to pay first."

"Don't worry," she said, stroking his arm, and the stocker's face went blank for a few seconds. "Do you keep a good supply of these?"

The stocker stared at her in wonder. "Just for Halloween."

Witchy Wanda turned pale. "Don't tell me this magnificent display celebrates that imposter holiday."

"Imposter?" The stocker looked confused.

"All-hallows, All Saints' Day, whatever you want to call it. A shabby substitution."

"For what? There's always been Halloween," the stocker said.

Witchy Wanda's eyes shone black. "The Celts had enough sense to understand that the new year begins with the end of harvest. On the eve of that new year, they burned crops and animals as sacrifices because they knew on that night the spheres of the dead and living mingle."

The stocker looked shocked. "It was lovely," Witchy Wanda assured him. She gestured at the packages of candy. "And these are used – how?"

The stocker looked even more shocked. "You don't know about trick-or-treating?"

"I've been away," Witchy Wanda said. "Do tell."

"Um," the stocker said, pushing the hair out of his eyes. "Little kids dress up in costumes and go to people's houses at night and say, 'trick or treat,' and people give them candy."

"What sorts of costumes? Ball gowns? Tuxedos?" She looked surprised when the stocker started rattling off a list including witches, ghosts, vampires and werewolves. "And the children come right to one's house, you say?"

41

"Not so much these days. A lot of times the kids just go somewhere for a Halloween party, like at the fire station."

"A flock of decorated children, all gathered together. Even better," Witchy Wanda said. "Oh, and would you show me where you keep jars and lids for canning? I'm making soup for winter. And I need a pepper mill, too."

Jackson slipped away. He'd heard enough to know that Mr. Dewey was right. An evil storm was brewing. And the name of that storm was Witchy Wanda.

Back in school the next day, Jackson got into more trouble for not paying attention. His mind just couldn't focus on adverbs and fractions when his gut was concentrating on Rodney. What if Rodney wasn't carrying that penny?

He'd be carrying the penny, all right. He'd taunt Jackson with it every time he had a chance. And that was the sum total of Jackson's plan: the moment Rodney flashed the penny, Jackson would pounce.

Jackson looked about to see what Rodney was up to. The miscreant was using a small round object to trace circles on a piece of paper with a pencil. He grinned at Jackson, held up the Indian head penny, and then returned to his activity. Jackson revised his plan. He would strike the first time he was out of a teacher's line of sight. At least now he knew Rodney had brought the lucky penny with him.

And it was lucky. Yesterday, Grandpa had been having one of his good days, and he told Jackson how he'd carried that penny all the way overseas and across battlefields. When Jackson asked what made it work, Grandpa had said faith made it lucky. Back in the old days, he said, for luck Celtic people carried pennies that they would turn over three times in their pocket at their first glimpse of a waxing moon. "Of course," he chuckled, "they also used to sprinkle salt in their children's hair to protect them from evil spirits." With his long white hair, Grandpa looked as Jackson imagined a Celtic king might appear, especially with those clear blue eyes that seemed to penetrate whatever they saw.

A flyer slapped on Jackson's desk by Mumps brought him back to the classroom. As Mumps circulated around the room at the teacher's direction, the kids began murmuring, then talking in more and more excited voices. Jackson looked at the bright yellow paper, which proclaimed that a genuine All Hallow's Eve celebration was to be sponsored by Ms. Wanda Lovecraft at her dwelling at 42 Crab Apple Street.

So that was what she was up to. Now he knew why she wanted all those jars and lids. She was planning on making quarts and quarts of kid soup. And he was sure she'd made up that last name.

When the teacher finally got everyone to shut up, he started rattling on about the history of All Hallow's Eve and how generous it was of Ms. Lovecraft to offer her home and how he was going to give extra credit to each student who attended. It was the most enthusiasm

Jackson had ever seen from Mr. Campbell, who mostly seemed irritated by the presence of his students. Some of the boys called him Cranky Campbell. But not the girls. They thought his dark hair and dark blue eyes made him handsome. Even the lines around his mouth and eyes, which Jackson figured came from all that work his face had to do smoking the cigarettes he'd seen him buying at the grocery, could not derail the females' admiration.

The intercom interrupted Mr. Campbell, calling Rodney to the office. Finally, some justice, Jackson thought with satisfaction. Whatever trouble Rodney was in, he deserved it.

"Oh, that's right," the teacher said. "You've got a dental appointment." Rodney swaggered out of the room with Jackson's penny.

After school, Jackson raced over to Dewey's department store. The next day was Saturday, the day of the celebration, and he was running out of time to extract the penny from Rodney. Maybe there was something in the suitcase that could help him.

"Mr. Dewey," Jackson said as soon as he burst through the door. "I was just wondering."

"Wondering what?" asked Mr. Dewey, arranging the men's handkerchiefs.

"How come this display case isn't shiny like the rest of them?" Jackson indicated the case closest to Miss Margot and her suitcase.

"Don't be ridiculous," Mr. Dewey said, but he walked over and inspected the piece. "You know, it could use a good polishing. A worthy task for you this afternoon." Mr. Dewey disappeared behind the black curtains that Jackson figured hid supplies and inventory, and the storekeeper did indeed reappear with polish and polishing cloths.

"Summon me if a customer needs assistance." Mr. Dewey must keep his office and records back there, too, to spend so much time hidden away.

Jackson opened the canister of cream polish, wrinkling his nose at the strong lemon smell. Dipping the cloth in the cream, he began polishing the case. After a few minutes, he extracted a tube of toothpaste from his back pack. He scrambled up onto the platform and pushed the suitcase away from the water stain. Just as Mr. Dewey had advised the day before, he carefully applied the toothpaste, then wiped it away. Next, he applied some of the lemon polish. Beautiful. No evidence left.

Not trusting his ears, Jackson stood and peered toward the curtains. No sign of Mr. Dewey. Jackson eased the suitcase onto the floor and opened it, lid facing the street in the rare event that a customer should walk by.

He couldn't believe it. The suitcase was filled with money. Enough money to buy a bicycle, never mind lucky pennies. Enough money to buy the newest game console. Enough – but it wasn't his money. Jackson started to close the lid, then reconsidered. What if he came up with a really great plan to defeat Witchy Wanda and needed supplies? And what was Miss Margot going to do with it, anyway? He stuffed some of the smaller bills into his pockets. Maybe he wouldn't even have to use it. And if he did, he'd repay her.

Jackson closed the suitcase. Then he opened it again and returned the money. He went back to polishing, wondering how a mannequin had accumulated so much money, if what she said was true. He also thought about Witchy Wanda, about Rodney, about the lucky penny and Grandpa's wacky story about sprinkling salt on kids. Suddenly, he sat back on his heels, an idea spinning around in his head.

Three Frankensteins sat at a card table set up on the sidewalk in front of Jackson's house. Jackson, who thought to himself with pride that he was the ugliest of the three, had recruited Leon and Alonzo from his class to help him with his enterprise.

He didn't really know the guys, just that Leon had the loudest mouth – and the best singing voice – in class. Alonzo was the king of drama. When he was in first grade, he'd been cast as a tree in a class play with one line, but he had turned it into a starring role. Despite the teacher hissing at him behind the curtains, he waddled into every scene in his tree costume, delivering his line over and over: "Behold my branches."

Leon looked like the one who should be an actor, with dark hair and serious brown eyes. Alonzo had dark hair and eyes, too, but he was a beefy kid who always looked like he had just heard a joke. If he pretended he was a fireman, though, you could practically see the flames he seemed to fight. He probably could fool real birds into thinking he was a tree.

Jackson figured they'd be perfect salesmen. He hadn't even tried to persuade Alonzo and Leon that Wanda Lovecraft was really a witch. He had simply tempted them with the promise of riches.

"Evil spirit protection," sang out Leon, like he was some opera star. "Get your evil spirit protection, right here."

"That is the dumbest thing I've ever heard," said a bright pink fairy. The princess and the two-legged black cat accompanying her giggled.

"Oh, is it?" asked Alonzo, the third Frankenstein. "Did you know that this is the time of year when the spheres of the dead and living mingle?" He had been well coached by Jackson. "Do you really want to take the chance of being snatched up by an evil spirit?"

"I guess not," the fairy relented. "How much?"

"Just one dime," said Jackson, who happened to know that Dr. Perez, the dentist who railed against sugar as the destroyer of teeth, gave out dimes instead of candy.

The fairy, the princess and the cat handed over their dimes to Alonzo.

"Now what?" the princess demanded.

Jackson stood. "Close your eyes."

The fairy pointed with her purple wand to the cat. "You go first and we'll make sure they do it right."

The cat, holding her tail in one hand and her treat bag in the other, reluctantly stepped forward. Jackson reached into his plastic pumpkin bucket and sprinkled the cat with a white powder.

"Hey," the cat protested, "What are you doing? What is this stuff?"

"A special substance, from a secret Celtic sea, from the land where Halloween was first celebrated."

The fairy evaluated the effect on the cat. "You know, it's kind of pretty the way you're glittering." And the next thing Jackson knew, the fairy and princess were arguing over whose turn it was to be sprinkled.

As the time drew near for the celebration, Jackson divided the money with the other Frankensteins, dropping his in a red vinyl bank deposit pouch his dad had let him borrow. The three Frankensteins headed for number 42. Jackson expected Witchy Wanda to be playing some scary sound effects, but instead he heard the happy sounds of fiddles, drums and bagpipes.

"What's in the bucket?" said a voice behind them. It was Rodney, dressed like a pirate.

"Evil spirit protection," said Leon, launching automatically into his sales routine before Jackson could think of how to react. "Want to buy some? Just a dime."

Rodney snorted, which made his black eye patch flap. "Pirates don't pay." He grabbed the plastic pumpkin from Jackson. "Evil spirit protection, right," he said. "What is this stuff? Sugar? Flour? Let's dump it and find out."

"Do so and suffer the consequences," said Alonzo. Jackson could tell he was shifting into his actor self. "You will not be the first fool to perish thusly."

If Jackson had called Rodney a fool, he already would have been lying on the ground. But Alonzo was sturdily built and looked like a fair match for a bully. "Kid stuff," Rodney said, shoving the bucket back at Jackson, who dropped the pouch to catch the pumpkin. The pouch dropped to the ground with a tinkle of metal. "Sounds like more coins for my collection," Rodney said, grabbing the pouch and running off.

Jackson fumed. He wasn't greedy – he'd come up with the idea of charging the kids to make the powder seem like something special, something everybody would want. But it wasn't fair that Rodney could just take the money.

"We going to let him get away with that?" Leon asked.

"We'll catch him when he's off guard," Jackson said, doubting, yet hoping, that such a thing might actually happen. But as soon as the

Frankensteins stepped inside the house, he momentarily forgot Rodney.

The three monsters stared in astonishment. The great room had been turned into a Halloween wonderland, lit by dozens of candles. Fancy-dressed waiters were wandering among the crowd of kids, offering trays of orange-frosted cupcakes. Buckets of candy had been placed on pedestals throughout the room, and Jackson saw his classmates rushing to fill their treat bags – and their mouths.

Witchy Wanda had been giving a lecture on the ancient art of soup making, allowing the pink fairy to stir the kettle of boiling water. Suddenly, she raised her head, and Jackson wondered if she sensed his presence. He hurried his buddies into the throng of partiers and Wanda turned her attention back to the cauldron.

Leon and Alonzo started helping themselves to chocolate mummies and marshmallow skeletons. As Jackson began walking casually to the punch bowl, he saw the bank pouch lying on the floor. He scooped it up and unzipped it. Empty. But at least he wouldn't have to explain the loss of the bag to his parents. Reaching the punch bowl, Jackson dumped the rest of the powder from his pumpkin. He picked up the ladle as though he were going to pour himself a drink and stirred the liquid thoroughly. He wondered how Witchy Wanda had paid for such an extravagant party.

"Cupcake, sir?" Jackson couldn't believe that the manager of the grocery store was working as a waiter. He looked around, recognizing the other waiters as clerks and stock boys. It came to him that all she'd had to do was look at their name tags and then zap them with a spell.

"No, thanks," Jackson said, though the cupcakes looked delicious. "But Ms. Lovecraft said she'd like a cup of punch." Quickly, he poured a glass of punch and handed it to the waiter, who dutifully carried it to Witchy Wanda. She frowned at his interruption and waved him away.

Now what? How in the world could he make her drink the punch? A gong sounded and Witchy Wanda left the fireplace, making her way to the center of the room. "I welcome you all to this All Hallow's Eve gathering," she said. "We're going to start with a fun game that I call, 'I cast a spell on you.'" She beckoned to the black cat. "What's your name?"

"Teresa."

"Teresa, I cast a spell on you." The cat froze in place, and the other kids laughed. Jackson knew they thought it was some kind of pretending game. Witchy Wanda pointed to the princess. "What's your name?"

"Jasmine."

"Jasmine, I cast a spell on you." The princess now stood motionless. Some of the kids shoved forward, shouting, "Me next! Me next!" Witchy Wanda obliged them.

Jackson wanted to yell that she was a witch and for everyone to run, but he knew that if he revealed himself, Witchy Wanda would manage to neutralize him and continue with her wicked plan. He had hoped the salt really would protect his classmates, but it seemed the story was just a legend. His last chance was to make Witchy Wanda drink the punch, but how?

Wanda pointed to the pink fairy. "Your name?"

But the fairy already had hypnotized herself. "You are so beautiful," she said, buzzing with sugar and caffeine. "When I grow up, I want to look just like you." She flung herself at Witchy Wanda, hugging her heroine. "You smell like flowers."

Witchy Wanda bent to return the embrace, her cheek brushing against the fairy's sparkling hair. "So sweet," she murmured. Then she sneezed. And sneezed again. "Contaminated!" she screamed. She coughed and clutched at her throat. She staggered over to the punch bowl, where a waiter hastily handed her a glass. She swallowed the drink. "That's better."

But it wasn't. Her bulging eyes found Jackson. "You." Her ears turned red. "You and I are not finished." She started to flicker, then shrink into a shiny black lump. Jackson scooped it up to the applause of the crowd. The fairy, the princess and the cat blinked as though they'd just awakened from a nap. The manager of the grocery store looked as though he wondered why he held a tray of cupcakes.

"Cool trick," one kid said. "How'd you do it? Where's the mirrors? When she's coming back?"

"Not tonight," Jackson said. "But she said for you to take home all the candy you want." That was enough to create a stampede. Jackson watched his classmates, including Rodney, snatching and grabbing.

He reached into his pocket and brought out an empty package for the organic Celtic sea salt. His mother had let him have the package after he'd begged that he needed it for class, which was sort of true, and after promising to do extra chores when she said that wasn't your cheap, chemically processed salt. Dropping the stone inside the bag, he returned it to his pocket and sought out Alonzo and Leon.

The three Frankensteins stood beside the train tracks. "We're not supposed to be here. What if the train's late?" Alonzo asked. He looked at the moonless sky. "It's gonna rain and ruin the candy."

"You sure you want to smash that rock?" Leon asked. "Won't she get mad? Aren't you supposed to give it back to her? Where'd she go, anyway?"

"I'm sure," Jackson answered. He was saved from further questions by the distant blast of a train whistle. "We'd better move."

Just then the patrol car of Officer Kearns appeared. The car stopped and the driver's window descended. "You boys are pushing curfew," he said. "Tell me you're headed home."

"We're headed home," Alonzo said. "Come on, Jackson."

"But–"

"We're headed home," Leon said. He and Alonzo muscled Jackson away from the tracks. At the sound of the next train whistle,

Jackson turned and had the satisfaction of seeing a passenger train bearing down on the stone formerly known as Witchy Wanda.

He allowed his buddies to steer him toward home. He'd return the next day for the remains. The police car followed them and pulled up beside them once again. "It's starting to rain," Officer Kearns said. "Get in and I'll give you a ride home." Alonzo and Leon dove inside the car, eager to protect their sugary loot.

Jackson turned his face to the sprinkling sky, thanking the clouds. Not one speck of light shone, not even from a peeping star.

While Jackson slept the sleep of one who has done his job, the rain stopped. The clouds drifted off to another destination. The moon appeared and smiled down upon a flat black disc lying on a railroad track. The stone began to glow before sparking into a black swirl.

Witchy Wanda sat up, her dress drenched, clutching her head. "What a hangover," she said aloud. "I feel like I've been bumpity-bump-bump-bumped." She stood up. She seemed taller than before.

She lurched down the street, staggering by Dewey's Department Store. Then she stopped, turned around and lurched back to the display window. "You haven't changed a bit," she said to the rigid form of Miss Margot.

And with a little giggle, Witchy Wanda began walking back to 42 Crab Apple Street.

54

Part Three: Missing Mumps

Jackson raced downstairs the morning after Halloween. He had to check the tracks and pick up the remains of Witchy Wanda before school. He wasn't sure yet how to dispose of her permanently, but he'd figure it out during school. He must pick a place where moon light could never, ever touch her.

Jackson found his parents in the kitchen, standing ready for A Talk. They had confiscated his Halloween candy. He was not going to gorge on it for breakfast the way he did last year, they informed him. This time, they were going to dole it out a few pieces at a time. They were not going to put up with him acting wild as a monkey on all that caffeine and high fructose corn syrup. In fact, they had worked out a schedule for dividing the candy so that he wouldn't finish it until Thanksgiving.

"Fine," Jackson said.

His parents then informed him they didn't need any attitude from him.

55

"No, really, fine," Jackson said. "Can I have my oatmeal now?" He wasn't about to eat that candy and make himself more snackable for any other witches that might be prowling around.

His parents eyed him with suspicion as he plowed through a bowl of oatmeal and drank an entire glass of orange juice. His father issued a warning: Don't even think about whining for candy just for eating a good breakfast.

"No time," Jackson said. "Got to get to school." He left behind two very bewildered parents.

Jackson arrived at the station to find a train stopped on the tracks, a line of coal cars stretching as far as he could see. No sign of a black disk. The train must be resting right atop the witch's dark heart.

"Lose another penny?" Jackson whirled to find Rodney and Mumps sitting on the railing of the station platform, watching him like a couple of young buzzards. "Loser's a good name for you," Rodney said.

"There's no such game as Loser," Jackson said.

Rodney howled and Jackson realized he'd misheard the insult. Rodney reached into his pocket and brought out the Indian head penny. "I've got a notion to send Liberty on a trip," he said. He slid off the railing onto the platform and wound up his arm as though he was going to deliver a pitch.

"Don't!" Jackson tried to jump from the ground to stop Rodney.

Rodney danced back and Mumps's pie crust face cracked with a grin of scorn. Rodney stuck the penny back in his pocket. "I think I'll keep it and try to sell it. I hear your grandpa collects coins."

Jackson froze. He didn't care now about how much trouble he got into with his parents, even if they never let him watch TV again. But he couldn't look at his grandfather's face, lined from years of struggle, and admit that he'd lost the penny that had been carried into war and back.

"How much do you want for it?" Jackson asked before he realized he didn't have any way of paying a ransom.

Rodney gazed down at Jackson and grinned. "I'll let you know." He and Mumps jumped from the platform. Rodney gave Jackson a shove that knocked him to the ground.

Clapping a hand over his ear to protect his hearing aid as he fell, Jackson curled into himself, expecting more. But Mumps said, "Come on, Rodney, we don't want Cranky Campbell catching us with the late bell."

Jackson raised his head, dislodging a piece of gravel nestled against his aching cheek and saw the scrawny black-and-white cat trotting toward him. He lay still as the cat approached him.

This was the first time he'd gotten a really good look at the animal, and now he noticed how most of its body was white, with black ears and black around the eyes and top of the head, like a mask. Black fur covered the top of the shoulders like a cape, extending part way down the forelegs. Even in his pain, Jackson could imagine the cat as a whiskered action hero. That would be awesome, truly. Truly awesome. Truly Awesome. What a great name.

Cautiously, Truly Awesome sniffed at him, perhaps hoping the human still held the chicken tender from their previous encounter. But when Jackson reached out his hand to pet the cat, it fled.

He stood and knocked the loose gravel from his clothes, rubbing his hand where a piece had punctured the skin. He limped into the station, only to discover from the station manager that it might be another hour before the train started moving again.

His hand bandaged awkwardly by the manager, who seemed suspicious of Jackson's claim to have fallen, Jackson walked on to school. (Technically, Jackson figured, he'd told the truth. He did fall. He just didn't tell the manager he was pushed first.)

He'd have to run back to the station after his last class and grab the stone – surely he'd find it on the track. Then he'd report for duty to Dewey's Department Store.

To make a bad morning totally rotten, he was late for school. Mr. Campbell told him he'd be spending recess in detention. Jackson noticed Leon and Alonzo were missing. He immediately worried that Witchy Wanda had gotten to them, but that was impossible. She was now a train track tortilla.

And then the rotten morning turned even more rotten when Mr. Campbell brought out a bunch of white boxes with gold lettering that screamed, "Classroom Candies Create Cash!"

"Fundraising time," Mr. Campbell announced.

Jackson hated school fundraisers. The school expected the kids to sell overpriced stuff to relatives and neighbors who really couldn't afford it. He still felt bad about the time he'd stopped at an old lady's house, trying to sell wrapping paper. "I could buy this for half the price at the dollar store," she'd said. Jackson had wanted to agree, but instead had said, "It's for the computer lab at school." So she reached in her purse. "I'm trying to save for an Amtrak ticket to go visit my sister, but I guess your school is more important."

Even worse, the school set up the fundraisers to pit the students and classes against each other. Jackson didn't care whether he won a stupid prize, but if he didn't try to sell and some other class won the bonus, Rodney and Mumps would be sure to punish him.

Jackson sighed to himself. Or at least he'd thought he'd sighed to himself. "Do you have a problem, Jackson?" asked Mr. Campbell.

"No, sir."

"Do I detect a lack of enthusiasm?" Mr. Campbell held up a Classroom Candies box. "Maybe you don't want to make the effort to sell a few candy bars to buy new playground equipment?"

"I was just wondering," Jackson said, before he could consider the wisdom of keeping his mouth shut, "why we don't raise the money with honest work." Jackson's grandfather talked a lot about honest work.

Everyone in the class went quiet, watching Mr. Campbell gripping the box of Classroom Candies. "And what do you consider honest work?"

"We could wash cars," Jackson said. "Or the windows on people's houses." He heard Rodney snort.

"We could have a bake sale," said Indira, a girl who almost never spoke in class.

"Yeah, right," Rodney said. "Like anybody's going to buy those potato pellets your mom makes."

"They're samosas, and they're delicious."

Mr. Campbell glared at them. "I do not recall opening the floor for a class discussion." He began passing out boxes. "Each of you should be able to sell at least one box of 20 bars in a week's time. Remember to tell your customers that we offer both the classic selection and the variety box, for those with special dietary preferences." He set aside two boxes. "I'm sure Alonzo and Leon will want to participate after they've recovered from their Halloween gluttony." That must mean they were home, having eaten themselves sick, Jackson figured. "The class member selling the most –"

"Go ahead and give me five boxes, Mr. Campbell," Rodney said. "I can sell a hundred candy bars, easy. Maybe more."

"An admirable goal," Mr. Campbell said, depositing five boxes on Rodney's desk. "As a further incentive, the class selling the most will receive a field trip to Crazy Frankie's World of Rides, with free rides all day."

As the class cheered, Jackson stared miserably at the box on his desk. He knew that if he didn't sell any bars and his class didn't win, everybody would be mad at him. And they'd know it was his fault, because the teachers made a point of posting classroom charts tracking each student's daily sales.

Jackson wanted to go to Crazy Frankie's World of Rides, too. The school's usual idea of a field trip was some dusty museum or a pumpkin patch. Crazy Frankie's, an hour's drive away, was the absolutely best amusement park. Jackson hardly ever got to go, because his parents said it was too expensive. Maybe he *could* sell a few bars. Maybe some people wouldn't mind the high price if it was for a good cause.

"Too rich for my blood," said the train station manager when Jackson held up a bar from his box. "Bet you can't afford one yourself. Here, have something from my stash." Jackson had gobbled the chocolate-and-peanut-butter treat before he remembered he was keeping himself pure from contamination. Then he relaxed, recalling that Witchy Wanda was just a flat black stone now, and he hurried outside to retrieve her from the track.

She wasn't there. He kicked through the gravel along the track. She had to be here somewhere. Jackson decided he'd stop on his way back from Dewey's Department Store. All he had to do was retrieve her before the moon came out.

Suddenly, Jackson felt eyes upon him. Dreading a resurrection of Double W, he looked around him, peering into the shadows of the train station. Then he relaxed. The eyes fixed upon him belonged to Truly Awesome.

Jackson withdrew a napkin from his pocket and unwrapped a piece of turkey he'd saved from lunch. Squatting, he held out the treat. The eyes blinked and then the creature moved forward. He remained still as the cat crept toward him. It stopped just short of his reach, sniffing the air.

Another motion from the shadows captured Jackson's attention. The fluffy cat from the police station leaped forward, grabbed the turkey in its mouth and sped away. Truly Awesome ran in the opposite direction.

"I think not," Mr. Dewey said when Jackson approached him about the candy bars. "I'd never stay in business if I charged such exorbitant prices."

Jackson wondered how Mr. Dewey could stay in business, anyway. Hardly anyone ever came in. Sometimes a tourist would walk from the train station to buy Glasglen post cards. Or someone might stop by to shop for a wedding gift. The girls from school would rush in to buy the latest book in some pony series, but the writer was very slow, and so far had produced only *The Pony in the Pines* and *The Pony in the Poplars*. Mr. Dewey must make most of his money at Christmas, Jackson decided.

Just then, the bell at the front door tinkled. Jackson turned to see a beautiful woman with dark eyes and wavy red hair, wearing a black robe. It couldn't be. It just couldn't be.

"What a marvelous establishment," said Witchy Wanda. "So charming, so quaint."

"Thank you, Madam." Mr. Dewey beamed with pride. Then the smile turned into a perplexed frown. "Have we met before?"

"I'm sure I would remember a gentleman such as yourself . . ." Wanda paused.

"Dewey. Martin Dewey." His brown eyes shining, he adjusted his wire-rimmed glasses and smoothed the fringe of white hair hovering over his ears.

"Some men have told me I'm unforgettable."

Jackson thought he would gag at her syrupy voice, but he stood rooted, waiting to see what happened next. He didn't think she would make a move on him without her kettle nearby.

"What do you have there, little boy?" Witchy Wanda asked, as if she didn't know his full name.

"Just some candy bars," Jackson mumbled.

"More accurately, an extortion scheme in the name of education," Mr. Dewey said, recovering his sourness.

"Oh, you're selling them?" From her tone of voice, Jackson had a feeling she already knew all about the fundraiser. "I'll take the box."

"What?" For just a few seconds, he was thrilled. Then he thought about how strong Witchy Wanda would become if she ate the entire box. "They're real expensive." He backed away, afraid she'd smell the chocolate and peanut butter on him.

Wanda reached out and grabbed the box from him. "Money is no concern to me." She reached into her robe and withdrew her vial of lily perfume. "But I do seem to be a bit short of cash." She dabbed a bit of lily oil on her wrists, and then smiled at Mr. Dewey as if she expected him to offer to buy the candy for her. But Mr. Dewey just stared at her with that trying-to-remember frown.

Wanda extended an arm to point at the storekeeper. "Martin Dewey, I cast a spell on you." Mr. Dewey went as rigid as Margot. "Been there, done that," Wanda said and walked over to the display window stage where Margot stood in her burnt orange suit beside her travel bag.

"Be a good boy and drag that suitcase down for me, will you?"

"What'd you do to Mr. Dewey?"

"Nothing I haven't done before," Witchy Wanda said. "Do you want to be paid for that candy or not?"

How did she know there was money in Margot's suitcase? "I'm not going to help you." He thought about trying to run out into the street for help, but he was afraid she'd grab him first. "You wouldn't really share any of the money, anyway."

64

Witchy Wanda sighed, stood on tiptoe and hauled the suitcase down from Margot's side. It dropped to the floor with a bumpity-bump-bump. Witchy Wanda considered the motionless mannequin for a second. "You're looking a bit peaked, I must say." Jackson could have sworn he saw Margot twitch, but that must have been his imagination. Wanda flung the lid open and began scooping up money and stuffing it into her pockets.

"That's stealing," Jackson told her.

"Not at all like a little boy borrowing something that doesn't belong to him, I suppose," Witchy Wanda said, stuffing away.

Jackson blinked. There was no way she could know about him almost taking money from the suitcase.

"What do you need all that for, anyway?"

Witchy Wanda smiled. "Children will be coming to my house wanting money for candy." She smiled even more. "I'll buy several boxes from one or two – I'll have to let them go, of course, to spread the word. And then the rest of the dears will troop right in, one after another." How dumb of her to tell him exactly what she was going to do. The moment she was gone, Jackson would warn all the kids in the school. He'd find some way to make them believe him.

Witchy Wanda stopped stuffing her pockets. She walked over to Mr. Dewey, still frozen, and plucked a key from his vest pocket. Witchy Wanda considered him. "If you don't open the store tomorrow, someone may call the police," she said to the impassive Mr. Dewey, who didn't even blink. "Then Officer Kearns will have to

65

force the lock. If you're found like this, unpleasant questions may be asked, especially if anyone noticed me walking in here." She held out her arm and pointed. "At the stroke of midnight, Martin Dewey, you may awaken."

"As for you," she said to Jackson, then paused. "I wonder–" she said. She strode to the back of the store and disappeared behind the black curtains. Jackson heard the screeching sound of something being twisted the wrong way on a machine.

Before Jackson could reach the front door, Witchy Wanda was there, blocking his exit. "Won't it be interesting when your boss finds you in his store in the middle of the night?" She slipped through the door. As she closed it, he heard a key turn.

Jackson raced to the door and pulled on it. Locked. Jackson groaned. No wonder Witchy Wanda didn't care whether he knew about her evil plan. Looking out the glass in the door, he saw Rodney coming down the sidewalk. Witchy Wanda reached into her gown, pulled out a wad of bills and traded them for Rodney's boxes of Classroom Candies. He just bet she was telling Rodney to send his schoolmates to her house. Jackson figured she'd have the whole school cooked by the time his parents missed him and came looking for him.

Witchy Wanda walked away, but Rodney stayed, counting the money with a big grin on his face. Jackson hated to do it, but he was going to have to appeal to Rodney. "Hey!" he yelled. "We're locked in. Go get help!"

Rodney looked suspicious. He tried the door and found it locked. Then he grinned. He reached into his pocket and brought out the Indian head penny, pecking it against the glass just to infuriate Jackson. He yelled back at Jackson. "Maybe I'll go see your grandpa." Rodney walked away and Jackson saw him meeting up with Mumps.

Jackson stood with his hand on the door knob, forgetting for a moment about Witchy Wanda. It would break his grandfather's heart to find out that Jackson had not taken better care of such a special gift.

"Let's get this mess cleaned up." Jackson whirled to find Miss Margot, alive and beautiful, shaking her head at the sight of the suitcase and scattered money.

"What we've got to do–" Jackson began.

"Is clean up this mess," Miss Margot insisted. Jackson found himself stuffing the money back in the suitcase as fast as he could. Then maybe she'd listen to him.

"Take a few bills for yourself."

Jackson reached for the money. If he could escape the store and find Rodney, maybe he could buy back the penny and his grandfather would never have to know anything about it. But something held Jackson back. Somehow, this didn't seem right. He withdrew his hand.

"Don't come begging for it later." Miss Margot snapped the suitcase shut. The two of them managed to hoist it back onto the stage. "And now we're going to pay a visit to Wanda Lovecraft. Right after I procure some medicinal herbs."

"You know her?" Jackson asked.

"Oh, yes, I know her."

"But we're locked in."

Miss Margot withdrew a piece of thin folded metal from her hair.

"What's that?" Jackson asked.

"It's called a bobby pin, and once upon a time it was a common hair accessory," Miss Margot said. She unfolded the bobby pin, walked over to the door and inserted it into the lock. "Very useful for tickling old-fashioned cylinders." She stepped back after prompting a couple of clicks. "Give it a try," she said as she refolded the bobby pin and returned it to her hair.

Jackson turned the knob and yanked open the door. "Let's go," he said, but he heard no reply. Turning, he saw Miss Margot had returned to her mannequin state. He looked over at Mr. Dewey, showing no sign of life, either. Quickly, Jackson dragged Miss Margot back to her stage, then rushed through the door, shutting it and running for his house. Somehow, he'd keep Rodney from showing Grandpa the penny, and then he'd figure out how to stop Witchy Wanda.

When he turned onto Crab Apple Street, he saw Rodney knocking at his door. But then he also spotted Mumps knocking on Witchy Wanda's door. Mumps was no friend of his – what did Jackson care if he ended up in a pot of soup?

Despite himself, Jackson found his feet headed for the witch's house. "Stop!" he yelled at Mumps just as the door opened.

"Find your own customers." Mumps gave Jackson a mean look. "Leave me alone."

Witchy Wanda looked surprised to see Jackson, but she spoke to Mumps. "Please come in."

Jackson tried to think fast. "She took a box from me, but she didn't pay me."

Mumps hesitated, but Wanda reached into the pocket of her robe and brought out a bunch of bills. Just as Mumps started to walk inside, Jackson tackled him, knocking the box out of his hands.

"Get off me," Mumps grunted, shoving Jackson aside. "Leave me alone." He picked up the box and held it out to Witchy Wanda.

Wanda grasped Mumps by the shoulder and quickly drew him inside. "I just need a receipt." She shut the door in Jackson's face and locked it.

He had to find Officer Kearns. Even if the officer wouldn't believe him, maybe he'd at least he'd go to the house and interrupt Witchy Wanda before it was too late for Mumps.

As he ran by his own home, the door opened and a deep voice said, "We need a word with you."

"But, Dad–" Jackson stopped to pant, out of breath from running.

"No buts." Jackson found himself hauled inside, to discover Rodney grinning, his father frowning and his grandfather giving Jackson an appraising look. Rodney was claiming to have found an

Indian head penny that Jackson's father recognized and now he wanted to know why Jackson had thrown away a valuable heirloom.

"I didn't throw away Grandpa's penny," Jackson protested.

Jackson's grandfather asked to see the penny, and Rodney handed it over, grinning. Jackson's father said the only way to be sure was for Jackson to go upstairs and bring his coin down to show them.

Grandpa held up his hand. "I'm not questioning Jackson's integrity. Are you?" Jackson's father finally answered no, sir.

Jackson's grandfather pocketed the penny. "But I'm always happy to add to my collection. Thank you, young man." He eyed Rodney. "Where did you say your regiment served?"

Rodney looked like he was in shock and Jackson's dad looked stumped. Jackson couldn't tell if his grandfather's mind had really slipped a gear, but he took advantage of the pause. "OK, great," he said, and dashed out the door. Jackson had wanted to tell his dad that something was wrong at the neighbor's house, but he figured he'd just waste time that Mumps didn't have, trying to persuade his dad that a witch was about to eat a bully burger.

Luckily for Jackson, but not so lucky for the driver pulled over, Officer Kearns was parked on Crab Apple Street, writing a traffic ticket. "Keep that speed down, buddy," Officer Kearns told the unhappy man. "Can't you see there are children on the street?"

Jackson saw swarms of kids marching down the sidewalks, clutching boxes of Classroom Candies. That rat Rodney must have told them that Wanda Lovecraft was in a buying mood.

Jackson ran up to Officer Kearns just as he was about to step back inside his patrol car. "There's a kid in there!" He pointed to Witchy Wanda's house.

Officer Kearns looked at him as though he were a pesky mosquito. "I imagine there will be a lot of kids going there," he said. "Ms. Lovecraft is a very generous woman."

"No, there's a kid in there, hurt," Jackson said. "It's Mumps. You have to save him."

"Not exactly one of your best friends, as I recall. You ever hear of the boy who cried wolf?" Officer Kearns asked, opening his car door. "Trust me, it doesn't end well for the boy."

Jackson saw the other kids advancing down the sidewalk, laughing and no doubt already planning their trip to Crazy Frankie's World of Rides. "Please," he begged, tugging at the officer's sleeve.

Officer Kearns whirled around and grabbed Jackson by the wrist. "You don't ever," he said in a harsh voice, "and I mean, ever, lay a hand on an officer of the law."

Without warning, tears sprouted from Jackson's eyes. "Please," he said again. "Please." He remembered the feeling of being boiled alive.

Officer Kearns released Jackson's wrist. "I'll go if you'll stop the waterworks," he said. "Too bad you don't have some of your grandfather's grit."

The words hurt Jackson more than the officer's grip on his wrist had. Jackson wanted to shout that he was worthy of his grandfather, that he had saved Officer Kearns from Witchy Wanda's stewpot. Instead, he followed the officer to 42 Crab Apple.

Officer Kearns knocked on the door. Jackson noticed him standing up straighter and re-tucking his uniform shirt inside his pants.

The door opened, sending out a wave of lily perfume, and there stood Witchy Wanda, smiling and looking more beautiful than ever. Her red hair shone. Her skin glowed a pretty pink. She looked like she had just taken an entire bottle of vitamins. She looked satisfied, too, the way someone looks after enjoying a really good meal.

But what Jackson couldn't believe was Wanda's belly, bulging under her black robe as though she were about to have a baby. Could witches have babies? If they did, he bet they'd be demon babies, with red eyes and hooves instead of feet.

Officer Kearns was staring, too. Jackson could see his face turn red as he realized Wanda Lovecraft had caught him staring. "Excuse me," he said. "I hadn't realized you were in the family way."

"What way?" Wanda caught up a lock of her red hair and twirled it around a finger as she regarded the officer and Jackson.

"You know, expecting." The officer's face offered an excellent imitation of a tomato.

"Expecting?" Witchy Wanda repeated. Then she said, "Oh, I see." She stopped twirling her curl. "I am not expecting anything, except the common courtesy of not having to endure comments on my personal appearance."

Now the face of Officer Kearns seemed to catch fire. "Pardon me," he said.

"I'm just suffering a bit of indigestion," she said.

"You haven't been eating clover or alfalfa, by any chance?" Officer Kearns asked. As one of Witchy Wanda's eyebrows raised, he quickly added, "Because it seems to me you've got more than a bit of indigestion. See, in sheep, sometimes they bloat because their food produces gas faster than they can digest."

Now both of Witchy Wanda's eyebrows stood at attention. "Are you comparing me to a sheep?"

"No, no," Officer Kearns said. "For one thing, you don't have green foam spewing out of your nose and mouth." When he saw Witchy Wandy's frown, he finished with, "But you might consider taking some mineral oil mixed with baking soda and water."

Jackson couldn't stand it any longer. "What about Mumps?" he asked.

Officer Kearns glared at Jackson, but he spoke to Wanda Lovecraft. "This witness claims there is an injured child on your premises."

"A boy did stop by to sell candy," Witchy Wanda said. "But there's no one here now."

"He never came out," Jackson insisted.

"Come inside and we'll discuss the matter." Witchy Wanda opened the door further.

73

Officer Kearns eagerly stepped through the doorway. Jackson started to follow, but the door shut in his face. Just as he was about to try the door himself, it opened once more. "I'm investigating your complaint," Officer Kearns said, scowling at Jackson. "Now go home." The door slammed.

Fine. He'd sneak behind the house and check the windows. But then he saw a bunch of girls from his class leaving the home next door and heading straight for the residence of Witchy Wanda.

The black cat, princess and pink fairy from the Halloween party marched right up to Jackson, trailed by Indira. "You can't go in there," Jackson said.

"Why not?" demanded Jasmine, the princess. "She's so rich, she can buy candy from all of us."

Jackson tried to think fast. "Go on, if you're not afraid of catching it."

"Catching what?" asked Teresa, the former cat, with a suspicious frown.

"The bloat."

"Ugh, what's that?" the pink fairy wanted to know.

"I'm not getting close enough to find out," Jackson told them. "All I know is that Officer Kearns talked about green foam coming out of her nose before he went in there."

"Eww," the pink fairy said, backing up.

"Really?" Indira asked.

"Really."

"I don't believe you," Teresa said, and proceeded to pound on the front door.

Jackson stepped behind a bush as Officer Kearns yanked open the door and glared at the girls. "What?"

The pink fairy, the princess and the cat screamed and ran. Peeking through the bushes, Jackson saw Indira look Officer Kearns straight in the eye. She reached into her box and held up a candy bar. "Classroom Candies?"

"No," the officer thundered and slammed the door. Indira looked thoughtfully at the bush where Jackson was hiding, then trotted after the other girls.

Jackson ran around to the back of the house, creeping through the shrubbery until he found the window from where he had once watched Officer Kearns bathing in Witchy Wanda's cauldron. The Queen Anne's Lace that had served him so well before had been dug up and removed. He arrived just in time to see Officer Kearns climbing the stairs behind Witchy Wanda. A few minutes later, when he saw her black boots starting back down the stairs, he dropped from the window, hoping she hadn't spotted him.

He waited a few moments, then cautiously raised his head just as the backs of the two adults disappeared down the steps to the basement. Jackson eased open the window just enough so he could hear their return, then dropped back into a crouch.

If Witchy Wanda hadn't hidden Mumps upstairs or in the basement, where could he be? And what was wrong with Witchy

75

Wanda to make her belly balloon? When the answer came to him, his legs collapsed and he found himself sprawled on the ground. She had eaten an entire child. No other explanation made sense.

"I hope you're satisfied," he heard Witchy Wanda say as she and Officer Kearns returned to what Jackson thought of as the stewpot room.

"I'm sorry to have bothered you, ma'am," Officer Kearns said.

"You don't have to be so formal with me," she said. "Call me Wanda." She reached out touched the officer's sleeve. "You know, I just love a man in uniform."

She couldn't be hungry, not after eating Mumps. That is, if she *had* eaten Mumps, and Jackson had a dreadful feeling that was exactly what she had done. But she must be about to commit some new act of evil to be acting so sweet to Officer Kearns.

Just then the blare of a car alarm began shrieking from the street. Officer Kearns seemed to come to himself. "Better check that out. Probably that McKinney kid messing where he shouldn't be."

Jackson fumed at the unjust accusation, but at least Officer Kearns headed out the door.

Witchy Wanda turned and strode over to the window. "That's right, go on home," she said as Jackson backed away from the window and prepared to run. She leaned out. "You cannot defeat me, Jackson McKinney. Men have tried and men have died attempting to vanquish me. Why should I fear a pup like you?" She smiled at him.

"In fact, I find it amusing that no one listens to the boy with the hearing aid."

Jackson sprinted around the house to the street, where he saw Officer Kearns talking to Rodney in front of a still-screaming sports car. Jackson kept running, and didn't stop until he reached his own house.

Inside, he found his parents wanting to know why he'd left when they hadn't finished talking to him and informing him he'd better start trying to get along with his classmates.

"I hope you don't plan on yammering until supper gets cold," Grandpa said, ending the lecture by shuffling his walker into the kitchen. His parents had replaced Grandpa's cane with a walker when he got confused once and thrashed the heads off all the tulips with the cane.

Jackson didn't think he could eat supper, but he found himself wolfing down brown rice and vegetables, figuring he needed the fortification. It was only a matter of time before Witchy Wanda went looking for another victim. Jackson thought his mother was going to fall off her chair when he asked for another helping of broccoli.

After supper, and after Jackson had finished his homework at the kitchen table, Grandpa beckoned Jackson to follow him into his bedroom. His grandfather eased himself into a recliner in the corner and motioned for Jackson to perch on the bed. "Do you know what integrity means?"

Jackson shook his head. "Not really. Is it kind of like honesty?"

"If you look in the dictionary, you'll find the word honest described as truthful, not deceptive. Having integrity means sticking to a code of conduct. Not exactly the same, is it?"

"No, sir," Jackson said, though he wasn't sure he understood. Maybe he hadn't been completely honest in not admitting right away the coin was his. But he thought he had integrity. He never tried to cheat on tests. He never picked on little kids.

"Now, what's this business about the penny?" Grandpa asked.

Jackson explained how he had lost the penny and that Rodney had gotten to it first. Jackson didn't tell Grandpa that Rodney had shoved him to the ground, but he saw Grandpa eying his cheek and hand.

"Sometimes you lose a battle, but you can still win the war," Grandpa said.

"What does that mean?" Jackson asked, wishing he could also tell Grandpa about Witchy Wanda. But if Grandpa did believe him and started talking about child-gobbling witches, Jackson was afraid his parents would drag Grandpa to the doctors again.

"Every time you lose a battle, you learn something about your enemy. Learn well, and you can eventually defeat your foe." Grandpa reached into his pocket, retrieved the penny and handed it to Jackson. "This is yours."

"What if I lose it?" Or what if it was taken from him again?

"It's yours to lose or keep," Grandpa said. "Good night, Jackson."

Jackson thought about his Grandpa's words as he brushed his teeth. He changed into his pajamas, turned out the light in his room and crawled into bed. He woke up the next morning still thinking about Grandpa's advice. He knew in his gut that Mumps was gone, but maybe he still had a chance to stop the rampage.

At school, he approached Mr. Campbell. "Could I get another box of Classroom Candies, the variety kind?"

"You *could* get another box if I permit you to do so. Your question, then, should be *may* I get another box?"

"*May* I get another box?" Jackson asked.

"Indeed you may." Mr. Campbell produced the requested product. "Glad to see you're getting into the sales spirit."

After school, Jackson rushed with the candy box to Crab Apple Street. How long would it take for a witch to digest a child? Was she already prowling again? He'd figure out later how to explain to Mr. Dewey why he didn't report to the store immediately after school. If his plan didn't work, he wouldn't have to worry about making excuses. He'd be the next item on Witchy Wanda's menu.

Just as he was about to knock, Jackson saw Indira watching him from across the street. She shook her head, like she was disappointed in him, and walked on. Jackson wanted to go after her, to explain that he wasn't try to steal a sale, but he knew there was no use. She wouldn't believe that he was trying to protect her from a kid-eating witch.

Witchy Wanda opened her front door before Jackson could even knock. She still looked a little plump, but nothing like the day before.

Crinkling his nose at the heavy smell of lily, Jackson plunged right into his memorized question: "Do you want to buy another box of candy?"

Witchy Wanda twirled a red curl of hair around a finger. "You're here to conduct business with me?" She seemed amused.

"I – I need the money," Jackson said.

"Come right on in," she said.

"I have to get back to the store," Jackson said. "Could you just give me the money now?" She might not be able to cast a spell on him because of his hearing aid, but she was still capable of grabbing him and stuffing him in her stewpot.

"That box looks different from the others."

"It's the variety box." Jackson opened the container and thrust a bar at Witchy Wanda. "Here, try one."

"I'm still rather full from my last meal," Witchy Wanda said. "But I do love my sweets." She reached into the pocket of her robe and brought out a few bills, offering them to Jackson. "Oh, go ahead," she said, when he hesitated to move closer. "I won't bite. At least not right this moment."

Jackson grabbed the money and stepped back, watching Witchy Wanda as she unwrapped the candy bar, shoving the whole thing in her mouth. Immediately, her eyes bulged and she began to cough and grab at her throat. "You–" she said, stopping to gasp. "You–" She flickered, then shrank into a black heart-shaped lump.

Jackson picked up the wrapper that had fluttered onto the doorstep. "Naturally sweetened with agave nectar. Absolutely no trans fats," it read. Too bad for Witchy Wanda that she had been too greedy to take the time to read the list of ingredients.

Jackson stuffed the stone in his pocket, took a deep breath and went inside the house. He began climbing the stairs, not wanting to, but maybe, just maybe, Mumps was up there and needed help. He found the rooms empty, not just of people, but of furniture, too.

Returning to the first floor, Jackson stood before the basement door, trying to will himself to finish his investigation. Double W was only a little black rock. Nothing in that basement could hurt him. Jackson's hand crept inside his pants pocket, checking to make sure that the stone was still there. His fingers also found the Indian head penny. If it could get Grandpa across battlefields, surely it could bring Jackson back up out of the basement.

He opened the door and flicked on the light switch. Nothing. No way was he going down into that basement without light. And what was the point? He was sure Double W had finished off Mumps. Still, Jackson turned away from the basement door and walked to the hall closet in the living room, looking for a new bulb. Then another thought prompted him to try the light switch in the living room. Again, nothing. Witchy Wanda didn't have electricity.

Jackson considered trying to sneak back into his own house to grab a flashlight. No, if Mumps was down there, Jackson didn't have

81

any time to waste. He returned to the basement steps again, leaving the door wide open to admit the sunlight from the great room.

Inching his way down the steps, Jackson called out, "Mumps?" No answer. At the bottom of the steps, Jackson peered into the gloom of the basement, making out the shape of a furnace and a water heater. No sign of Mumps. When a spider scuttled across his shoe, Jackson yelped and raced back up the steps and out of the house.

Starting down the street, Jackson stopped, reached into his pocket and brought out the stone and the Indian head penny. He'd use Grandpa's luck to make sure the witch's had run out. Before the moon shone again, he'd get rid of her for good. "Double W," he said, cramming the stone and penny back in his pocket and continuing down the street, "No more stew for you."

Part Four: Carnival

With a dead witch and a lucky penny in his pocket, Jackson hurried to report for duty at Dewey's Department Store. Mr. Dewey winced as the bell on the door jangled. "Keep it to a dull roar, will you, McKinney?" he said, not even mentioning Jackson's tardiness. "I have a headache. I don't know what possessed me to work so late last night." The white fringe around his ears stood on end like someone had rubbed his hair with a balloon. His wire-rimmed glasses sat askew on his nose and he looked at Jackson with dull brown eyes.

"What do you want me to do?" Jackson asked, hoping Mr. Dewey would set him to a task and disappear behind the black curtains.

"I need you to change the window display for me." Jackson could hardly believe his luck. "I was going to do it myself, but I just don't feel up to it today." He gestured to a pair of engineer's boots and a pile of clothing topped by a cap that looked like the kind train conductors wore, except that this one was firecracker red. And made of velvet.

Jackson stood in shock. Miss Margot had worn the burnt-orange suit ever since he could remember. "But she always wears the same outfit."

"Recent circumstances have led me to the conclusion that I must update my marketing," Mr. Dewey said. "A national railroad society is taking a fall train tour that includes Glasglen, and I need to draw new shoppers. So hop to it."

Reluctantly, Jackson picked up the pile of clothing. He had a bad feeling about this wardrobe change. As he walked by Mr. Dewey's counter, he saw that the old man would stand for a few seconds on one leg, then shift to the other. Jackson struggled to keep himself from smiling at Mr. Dewey, who looked like a skinny crane. He guessed his feet would hurt, too, if he'd been standing for hours under a witch's spell.

Mr. Dewey limped to the rear of the store. "I'll be in the back should a customer need assistance." He vanished behind the black curtains, but popped back out almost immediately. "My equipment!" He pointed a finger in accusation at Jackson. "You ruined my equipment."

"What equipment?" Jackson said. "Besides, you're the one that's been in the store. I just got here."

"Oh," Mr. Dewey said, now looking extremely puzzled as well as angry. "Well, carry on." Once more he vanished behind the black curtains.

Jackson was mightily tempted to follow to see just what sort of equipment lay behind the curtains, but instead he rushed over to the display stage. Setting the clothing on the suitcase, Jackson stood, trying to figure out what could be the connection between Rodney pecking on the display window and Miss Margot coming alive. Both times Rodney had used Grandpa's lucky coin. Jackson rummaged in his pocket, fingering the cold stone that had once been Witchy Wanda, and brought the Indian head penny out of his pocket. He tapped the coin against the glass. Nothing. He closed his eyes, trying to remember the particular rhythm, and tried again.

Miss Margot's hard plastic features softened and her pale blue eyes blinked, her lashes fluttering against her cheeks. Before she could speak, Jackson thrust the clothes at her. "Hurry, you have to change, and then we can talk."

Miss Margot shook out a pair of pin-striped overalls, regarding them, the boots and the red cap with disdain. "Absolutely not."

"You have to," Jackson said. "If you don't, Mr. Dewey will make me do it."

Miss Margot looked horrified. "You wouldn't!"

"It's the latest fashion," Jackson said, worried that Mr. Dewey could walk out at any moment.

"Truly?" Miss Margot said with doubt in her voice.

"Truly," Jackson said.

Sighing, Miss Margot stepped from the stage and disappeared into the women's changing stall. She emerged wearing the overalls and the red cap set on her head at a jaunty angle. From a sales table, she plucked a scarf patterned with diamonds of purple, blue and red and wound it around her neck. "That's better," she said.

"Come back to the window," Jackson said in a whisper.

"Why?"

"So Mr. Dewey can't hear us."

And just like that, she turned plastic again. Jackson considered tapping the penny against the nearest display case, but he was afraid that would rouse Mr. Dewey's attention. He wrestle-walked Miss Margot back to the display window. Looking out the window, he saw the fluffy cat chasing Truly Awesome down the street, out of sight. He was just about to try the code again when his mother strolled into the store.

"Mom, what are you doing here?"

His mother replied that it was a free country, and she guessed she could walk into any retail establishment she wanted. When Mr. Dewey emerged, drawn by the sound of the bell, she explained that she thought with the evenings getting chillier she'd start picking up Jackson. But Jackson knew she had the missing Mumps on her mind.

"A worthy effort," Mr. Dewey said, nodding at Miss Margot. "Nice touch, the scarf."

Sighing, Jackson returned the penny to his pocket and followed his mother out of the store. He'd have to learn the mystery of Miss Margot later.

The debate raged more furiously than the flames, which hadn't even started yet. All Jackson had done was to ask if he could be the one to build the fire for the McKinney family's end-of-warm-weather weenie roast. He was, after all, a witch slayer.

His parents, however, did not know that. Absolutely not, his mother said. Maybe next year, if he proved himself responsible, his father said.

Grandpa ended the argument by opening a kitchen cabinet and reaching for a box of matches. "Those hot dogs don't look like they're getting any younger," he said, eyeing a platter of grayish sausages on the kitchen counter.

"They're uncured turkey dogs," Jackson volunteered. "No nitrates." Once Jackson would have gagged at the sight of the turkey dogs, but it wouldn't hurt to avoid the chemicals in processed foods, at least until Double W was gone for good. The stone that had once been Witchy Wanda rode in his pocket.

Grandpa shook his head at the turkey dogs and handed the box of matches to Jackson. Before Jackson's parents could protest, Grandpa said, "Carry these for me," directing his walker out the door.

Jackson followed his grandfather outside, then fetched a few sticks of firewood and some slivers of kindling from a small shed. He set to work in the gravel pit the family used for cookouts, constructing a pyramid with the firewood. Surely his parents couldn't object to that. Then he began arranging the kindling, which reminded him of chopsticks, around the bigger hunks of wood.

His grandfather held out the box of matches. "Let's get this show on the road."

Jackson grabbed the box. If his parents had a problem, they could take it up with Grandpa. Jackson struck a match against the side of the box, then held the flame to a stick of kindling. The match burned down to his fingers as he tried to use it to light another piece of kindling. Dropping it, he sucked on his fingers, then set back to work. Several matches later, the dry kindling was burning and beginning to spread over the firewood.

Jackson felt in his pocket for the stone. He needed to pitch it into the fire, but he didn't know what he could say to Grandpa without having to explain himself. But his grandfather was staring away from the fire. Quickly, Jackson yanked the black heart from his pocket and flung it into the deepest part of the fire. If coal burned to ashes, so would Double W.

He looked toward his grandfather, who still stood staring at nothing in particular that Jackson could see. "Grandpa?" he said.

Jackson's father emerged from the house, catching Jackson with the box of matches. Just as he was beginning to launch into a lecture, Grandpa snapped at him. "Douse that fire, soldier. You want to announce our position?" Jackson's father hurried toward them, a look of concern on his face that had nothing to do with matches.

Grandpa looked at Jackson, his pale blue eyes seeing someone else. "What is that child doing here? Get him out of here."

"Grandpa, it's me," Jackson said, laying a hand on his grandfather's where it gripped the walker. The hand was roughened from work and age. For just a second, Jackson thought his grandfather was going to fling his hand away, maybe even hit him. But then he seemed to come to himself.

"Of course it's you," he said. "Bring on the turkey dogs."

Later, Jackson received the parental speech about how Grandpa was going to have these moments of confusion and Jackson had to learn to be more responsible. The lecture ended when Jackson wanted to know why doctors couldn't do something for Grandpa and his parents said not every problem had an answer.

Jackson thought about that over the next several days, with the class buzzing about the extended absence of Mumps. His parents had appeared on the television news, weeping and begging for viewers to contact them with any information. Officer Kearns told reporters he believed the boy had run away. Sitting at his desk, trying to concentrate on Mr. Campbell, Jackson knew there was no point in telling the adults that a witch had gobbled Mumps. At least she couldn't hurt any more children.

Suddenly, his stomach churned. He'd forgotten all about Double W when Grandpa had what his parents called an episode. But she had to be toasted charcoal. After Grandpa came back to himself, they'd roasted turkey dogs and organic marshmallows. Double W must be ashes by now. Still, he'd check out the gravel pit when he got home from Dewey duty.

"Jackson," Mr. Campbell said. "How long would you say high-speed communications have been available?" Mr. Campbell, impatient for Jackson's answer, ran a hand through his dark hair, a gesture that made Halloween princess Jasmine and the pink fairy sigh as happily as if they'd been given a copy of *Pony in the Pines* autographed by the author.

"Since computers?" Jackson guessed. "Since cell phones?"

"Reach back further," Mr. Campbell said. "More than a hundred years ago, Samuel F.B. Morse created a code of dots and dashes, or dits and dahs–" The class interrupted him with laughter. Mr. Campbell raised an eyebrow that settled the group and continued. "This code was relayed by telegraph lines, radio circuits and undersea cables." He handed out copies of a Morse code alphabet chart. "Try translating this message."

Jackson looked around the room. Leon seemed bored. Alonzo looked tired, like he'd stayed up late again trying to become the youngest actor ever to memorize Shakespeare's plays. Rodney looked lost, as though he couldn't be himself without Mumps. Jackson almost felt sorry for him, but then he remembered the shove at the railroad station. Indira frowned, concentrating on copying the correct sequence of dots and dashes.

"Waiting for inspiration, Jackson?" Mr. Campbell inquired.

"No, sir." Jackson bent to his paper. Dash, dash, dot. "G." Dash, dash, dash. "O."

He had finished the first word. He was about to proceed to the next when he paused. There was something familiar about that pattern. Dah, dah, dit, pause. Dah, dah, dah. A memory played in his head of the sound of a coin tapping against glass. He stared at his paper, astonished. That miscreant Rodney had accidentally tapped a spell-breaking code that had awakened Miss Margot. And in trying to duplicate Rodney's actions, Jackson had activated the code, too. He still couldn't understand why she kept freezing up again, but now he could talk to her whenever he wanted. He couldn't wait for school to end so he could head for the store. Then he remembered that his mother was picking him up after school for a haircut.

The intercom crackled and the vice principal's voice announced, "Hey, sorry to intrude, dudes. This is the VP here." The class laughed. The only way of guessing the vice principal had graduated from college was the necktie he wore. Some of the parents complained that his only credential was being the school board president's nephew, but all the kids liked him.

"We know you've been waiting to find out who won the trip to Crazy Frankie's World of Rides." The laughter ceased and every pencil paused. "Congratulations to Mr. Campbell's class!" The room erupted in cheers. Jackson noticed that Rodney didn't even react. But it was hard to feel sorry for a bully.

91

Over the intercom, the class could hear the principal telling the vice principal to get on with it. "Thing is," the voice in the box said in a tone that promised bad news was coming. "It's not exactly a trip to Crazy Frankie's." Alonzo and Leon already were starting to look outraged. "Seems there's some sort of liability concern–"

The groans from the class must have drifted down the hall, because the vice principal rushed on. "The good news is Mr. Campbell's class will be exempt from classes all day Friday to attend the harvest festival."

Jackson hadn't wanted to sell the stupid candy in the first place, but even lamer was winning a trip to a festival in his own town. A day out of school was something, but in past years he'd already gone on the hay ride around the old high school football field and threaded his way through the corn maze.

"I got one word for you, dudes," the vice principal said. "Carnival."

Carnival! They'd never had mechanical rides at the harvest festival before.

"A real carnival, dudes. Whirl 'til you hurl." Suddenly the intercom went dead, no doubt silenced by the principal.

Naturally, it would pour rain on the day Jackson's class was supposed to celebrate its Classroom Candies victory. The only good thing about it was that it would drive Witchy Wanda's ashes deep into the ground. Jackson had found no evidence of a black heart in the remains of the weenie roast fire, so it was good riddance to Double W.

Mr. Campbell herded them aboard the bus that would take them across town to the old high school. Jackson had the misfortune not only to be seated beside a girl, Indira, but also to be located in front of Rodney, who immediately started kneeing him in the back.

Maybe he should have brought his lucky penny, but Jackson had decided the night before that a school outing would give Rodney too many chances to steal the coin from him again.

The knee repeatedly slammed into his back, but Jackson tried to ignore it. Then Rodney, who was enjoying a seat all to himself, slid over and began giving the same treatment to Indira. Mr. Campbell, seated way up front, was occupied in talking to the driver. Jackson watched Indira grimacing as her head bobbed back and forth, her dark braid swinging like a rope, then whipped his own head around. "Cut it out," he said.

Rodney grinned at him. "You gonna make me?"

Before he could consider the craziness of challenging a bully, Jackson answered, "Yeah, I'm gonna rake you."

Rodney roared and Jackson realized his hearing aid had failed him. As the kids around him snickered, he could feel his face growing hot. The knee dropped when Mr. Campbell stood to survey the commotion. "Don't worry," Rodney said. "I'll settle up with you later."

Jackson slumped in his seat. He might be a witch slayer, but only a nut would take on Rodney.

"Don't worry," Indira said in a low voice. "I'll tell Mr. Campbell."

"Don't," Jackson said. "I'll take care of it." How, he didn't know.

Arriving at the high school, Jackson and his classmates trooped through the rain past the rides and into the gym, which had been turned into a carnival midway. Mr. Campbell assured them that if the sun came out, the rides would resume. In the meantime, they could play all the games they wanted – no charge. Plus, free cotton candy for everybody.

Jackson immediately dug into his mound of feathery blue sugar. With Double W gone, he could enjoy himself. And his parents didn't have to know about his indulgence. What happened at carnival stayed at carnival.

Rodney trod on Jackson's foot as he headed for the baseball pitch. "Excuse me, Jackson."

Jackson winced, but said nothing. Indira, standing nearby, said, "I should tell Mr. Campbell."

"Don't," Jackson said. "It'll just make things worse."

Indira looked as if she wanted to argue with him, but didn't. Watching the other kids scatter to the games, she said, "That day with

94

the candy bars, why did you go back to Wanda Lovecraft's house after telling us to stay away?"

Surprised, Jackson couldn't think of an excuse. "I, I–"

"You wanted us to go away so you could sell more, right?" Indira stared at him with eyes as dark as Leon's and Alonzo's, but much more serious.

"No–"

"I didn't think so." Indira folded her arms. "You think there's something fishy about Wanda Lovecraft, don't you? Me, too. I saw you talking to that policeman."

Jackson didn't know what to say. It'd be a relief to have someone to talk to, but he doubted Indira would believe Double W was a witch. And what was the point now? The story was finished.

Before he could invent some sort of answer, the princess, fairy and cat came along and swept up Indira. "Let's go to the fortune teller!" the princess Jasmine said, leading the pack of girls to a black tent sitting in a corner of the gym.

Jackson shrugged and headed for the basketball hoop. Maybe he could win the big pink bunny for his mom. Leon, having failed to sink even one shot, rejoined the line behind Jackson. "That thing is rigged," he said.

"So how come you're still in line?" Jackson asked.

"Statistics, my man. That ball is going through the net for somebody."

"Not if you keep trying to bank it off the backboard," Jackson said.

Alonzo, standing in front of Jackson, turned around and asked, "How come?"

"I read somewhere that they put more air in the balls so they'll bounce right off the backboard," Jackson said. "Don't aim for the rim. Shoot it like this." Jackson pantomimed a high arch.

"Sooooome wheeeeere over the rainbow," Leon began singing.

"I'm going for my patented bank shot," Alonzo said. When he, too, bombed out, he stepped aside and said, "Let's see your rainbow shot."

Jackson planted his feet firmly on the floor. He bent his knees, then sprang up, releasing the ball in a high arc, watching it descend into the basket.

Leon whistled. "Nothing but net."

Jackson did it again and again. Grudgingly, the operator rewarded him with a pocket knife. "What does it take to win that?" Jackson asked, pointing to the rabbit.

"You can trade three medium prizes for a big prize," the operator told him.

Jackson started to return to the end of the line, but then thought of how handy it would be to own a knife, even if he couldn't carry it to school.

With the knife in his pocket, Jackson felt lucky again. Maybe Rodney would back off if he saw Jackson was armed. He looked around the gym. Rodney was still at the baseball pitch, stewing about having to wait his turn. Jackson walked in the opposite direction, toward the shooting-star booth. His parents wouldn't let him have his own BB gun.

As he neared the booth, Jackson saw the girls emerge from the black tent. He expected them to be giggling over the fortune teller's predictions, but they emerged silently, floating along as though – *as though they were under a spell.*

With a sinking feeling, Jackson approached Indira. "What'd the fortune teller say?"

Indira's brown eyes looked glazed. "We're going to find great treasure."

"Where?"

"It's a secret."

"You can tell me," Jackson said.

Indira wobbled a little where she stood. "Don't tell anybody else," she said. "It's 42 Crab Apple Street. We're going right after school."

Double W's house! "Don't do it," he warned. "It's a trap."

Indira frowned. "You just want the treasure all for yourself, just like you tried to keep us from selling our candy."

No use trying to reason with her. Jackson took a deep breath and plunged into the tent.

Jackson had expected to find Double W perched on a folding chair at a card table, with some sort of cheap crystal ball. Instead, he found himself enveloped in a vast dark space. Impossibly, stars twinkled overhead. Also impossibly, a slight breeze blew, carrying the gagging smell of lily. He glanced back to mark where he had entered, but saw nothing but blackness. Light from the gym should have been peeping beneath the tent, but there was only darkness.

Turning back to the interior of the tent, Jackson made out a sitting shape. A small globe began to glow in a soft pale hand. The glow grew, revealing Witchy Wanda comfortably seated in a huge stuffed chair that had arms ending in snarling wooden lions' heads. In the light of the globe, her red hair seemed to be burning.

"You desire to learn your fortune?" she asked.

"You—you can't be here," Jackson said. He stood where he was, well out of snatching range.

"My presence would seem to indicate otherwise." Her free hand stroked one of the lion's heads.

"But I barbecued you." Jackson knew he was babbling. He needed to stall for time to figure out his next move. He considered the knife in his pocket, but Double W might snuff out the light and gain the advantage if he attacked her. He wasn't even sure if he could bring himself to actually strike. It was one thing to think about waving the knife in front of Rodney; it was another to do violence to another being, even one as evil as Double W. Even though Grandpa had been to war, he had said that violence begat violence.

"I have your safety-minded father to thank for my resurrection." Double W smiled genially. "He returned to the scene of your crime with a bucket of water and gave me a good soaking. Then the moon very considerately shone upon me."

Jackson wanted to groan. He'd been on enough camping trips that he should have known that was exactly what his father would do.

Double W stopped petting the lion's head. "Now, pay attention, because this is the last time I'll ask: Do you wish to learn your fortune?"

"Sure," he said, continuing to stall for time. "What do I do? Look into that ball?"

She ignored his question. "Forward or reverse?"

Despite his fear of standing in an impossibly sealed tent with a kid-eating witch, Jackson asked, "What would be the point of going backwards?"

Witchy Wanda smiled at him, tossing the globe lightly from hand to hand. "Why don't you find out?" Rising, she turned and threw the ball into the darkness behind her. "Fetch."

Two fears battled quickly within Jackson. The globe hurtled into a void that shouldn't even exist. But as it sped away, the space between Jackson and Double W grew darker. His hearing aid might protect him from a spell, but if she could sneak up on him, she could simply seize him and head straight for the stewpot. Jackson smelled her lily perfume drawing closer.

The ball stopped, suspended in the air, as if waiting for Jackson's decision. He ran after it, the lily perfume following. As soon as he began running, the globe sped away from him. Jackson thought his lungs would pop as he pumped his arms and legs as hard as he could. The ball bobbed ahead, but Jackson gained on it. He reached out a hand, his fingers closing around his catch.

The moment he touched the globe, Jackson felt himself shifting inside. His feet no longer touched anything solid. He hurtled through the blackness, finding himself deposited in a brightly lit living room that looked exactly like his own. A toddler played on the floor, his parents standing over him.

"Couldn't they just fix him with an operation?" That was Jackson's dad, with more hair on his head than he sported now.

"You know they said the hearing loss wasn't extensive enough to risk surgery." His mom looked slimmer.

"But he'll always be different."

"Everyone's different, in some way," his mother said.

Jackson felt the rustle of a slight breeze and smelled lilies again before he heard the voice. "Do you perceive now how you can see your future by stepping backwards?"

Jackson turned to find Double W standing beside him in her black robe, smiling. He wanted to dart away, then considered the fact that he still didn't seem to be standing on anything firm. Tentatively, he reached out to touch her sleeve. His hand dipped right through the fabric, feeling nothing.

"We're not really here," Jackson said. "You're messing with my mind."

"I am indeed messing with your mind," Witchy Wanda said. "Predators always like to play with their prey." She brushed at her sleeve as though his touch had contaminated her. "To clarify, your consciousness is here while your body remained behind. Take care with your little toy – drop it and you'll never return."

Jackson gripped the globe as tightly as he could. "My parents never really said that stuff." But he knew, deep inside, that they had. And his dad was right – Jackson had always felt different.

"The condemned prisoner always receives a last request," Double W said. "I'll grant you one more visitation."

"I'm not your prisoner," Jackson said. He thought once more about the knife in his pocket, but a knife slicing through thin air wouldn't do him much good.

Witchy Wanda smiled so pleasantly that Jackson felt his stomach shrivel. "Indulge me, then."

"The suitcase in Dewey's Department Store," he said. "Where'd that money come from?" As soon as the words had left his mouth, he wanted to kick himself. He needed to find out so much. Why'd he pick that dumb question?

Wanda cocked her head and considered him. "Interesting choice," she said.

Jackson wasn't even aware of blinking, but suddenly the living room had disappeared, replaced by Dewey's Department Store. Except it wasn't exactly the store Jackson remembered. There was no mannequin in the display window, just pots of flowers. The clothes looked different, as out of style as Miss Margot's burnt orange suit. This must be the past, years and years ago.

As he watched, Miss Margot – looking very much alive – and Witchy Wanda walked into the store. They each held the hand of a little blond-haired boy, maybe two or three years old. In her free hand, Miss Margot carried the suitcase that usually sat in the display window. Jackson wanted to grab the kid and run, then remembered that everything he saw already had happened long ago. Miss Margot wore her burnt orange suit, Double W her usual black garb. The little boy slipped away from them to pounce upon a toy train.

Jackson sputtered, "You acted like you hadn't been to Glasglen before."

"I did, didn't I?" She watched the little boy with the train. "I thought we'd never drag him away from the telegraph operator at the station."

Jackson realized then that Double W could have been lying, too, about the bucket of water saving her from the barbecue. Maybe the fire hadn't even touched her black heart. Maybe it was just the moonlight that had saved her.

Just then a very young Mr. Dewey – Jackson wondered why the women didn't look younger, too – emerged from the back of the store.

"Is that the lad?" he asked.

"Woo-woo," the little boy said, pushing the train along the floor. "Wook, Auntie," he said to Double W. When she didn't respond, he called to Miss Margot, "Wook, Auntie."

One of Mr. Dewey's eyebrows arched in speculation.

"We are cousins to each other, and to his mother, may she rest in peace," Double W explained. "It seemed easier to have him call us Auntie."

"His father?" Mr. Dewey asked.

"Died in service to his country," Double W said. "So many do. Let us proceed. I've got a train to catch."

"*We've* got a train to catch," Miss Margot said.

Mr. Dewey walked to the back of the store and drew aside the curtains. "Enter, ladies."

"Come, boy," Double W said. The little fellow picked up the train and trotted after them.

The front of the store dissolved away and the back room unveiled itself. A brand-new machine was spewing green slips of paper. Next to it sat several stacks of money. Miss Margot sat the suitcase down, opened it, and stuffed the bundles inside. "Nothing but small bills," she complained.

"Small bills are seldom questioned as counterfeit," Mr. Dewey answered.

Miss Margot snapped the suitcase shut. "Done."

"There is the matter of my compensation," Mr. Dewey said. "It wouldn't do for me to spend any of this–" He pointed to the percolating press. "—until I'm ready to leave town."

"The gold, yes," Double W said, walking out of the back room toward the counter. Miss Margot followed, suitcase in one hand, the other holding the hand of the blond boy. Mr. Dewey trailed behind them.

Counterfeit. Jackson thought about the money Witchy Wanda had confiscated to buy all those candy bars. That money was gone, but maybe he could do something to stop Mr. Dewey. If he lived.

The past Double W reached inside her robe pocket as though rummaging for the payment. Instead she drew out a hand and pointed at the storekeeper. "Martin Dewey, I cast a spell on you." Mr. Dewey went rigid. The little boy wriggled out of Miss Margot's grasp and ran up to the human statue. He stuck out his tongue and laughed when he got no response.

Miss Margot looked at him fondly. "He's a sweet boy. Can't we keep him? He might have some portion of The Gift."

Double W looked at the boy, who was wiping his nose on his sleeve. "Not a drop."

"Still, it might develop," Miss Margot argued. "Let's take him back."

"I've tolerated enough of your foolishness," Double W said. "I allowed you to keep that rabbit that I should have thrown in the stewpot. And I've let you play healer while I've been teaching you the properties of herbs."

"Healing can be part of The Gift–"

"Martin Dewey," Double W said, as though Miss Margot hadn't spoken, "You are not leaving town. When you awaken in half an hour, you will remember nothing of this transaction. You *will* remember ordering Margot the mannequin."

"I'm not sure I want a mannequin named after me," Miss Margot said, then stopped, her eyes blinking with nervousness. "Wait a minute. You wouldn't–"

"I would," Double W said. "Margo, I cast a spell on you." Miss Margot went rigid, like Mr. Dewey. "I'm worn out with you always trying to persuade me to eat lentils instead of children. The Gift must be fed." She reached out and touched Miss Margot's cheek, which grew cold and plastic, as did the rest of her body. "I leave you the present of eternal youth." Double W lugged Miss Margot and the suitcase over to the display window.

Jackson couldn't believe what he was seeing. "You double-crossed her!"

Witchy Wanda grinned as though he'd paid her a compliment. "Nicely done, if I do say so myself."

"Why'd you leave the suitcase when you came all the way for the money?"

"That was Margot's idea, to pay for the boy's care at some home or institution. I never had any intention of actually enrolling him in a facility. Entirely too complicated."

"Then why'd you come to Glasglen at all? Why didn't you just kill them, like you tried to kill me?"

Double W seemed shocked. "That would be poor manners. This was a very tidy solution to a troublesome situation."

Jackson turned back to the unfolding scene. "Come, boy," Double W said to the child. He scooped up a penny he had just found on the floor and stood, clutching the train to his chest.

Double W plucked the train from him and returned it to its shelf. As she bent, a ball rolled from her pocket, unnoticed by Double W or the boy focused on the train. The ball rolled all the way past the black curtains.

Jackson realized then that she had found the globe years later when she returned to the store the day he'd shown up with the candy bars.

"Orphans don't arrive with accessories," Double W now told the boy. The little fellow's face puckered at being robbed of his pleasure. "Don't cry," she said. "We're going to see a big train."

"Big train," the boy repeated. Somewhat mollified, he followed her out of the store, pausing to peck on the display window with his penny. "Go," he said to his motionless cousin. Double W, looking down the street at the approaching passenger train, didn't notice Miss Margot's eyelashes flutter. "No, she has to stay," Double W said. The fluttering ceased.

Jackson gaped. It was the boy who had cast the wake-up spell. Could he have known Morse code? Did he do it by accident? Or did he have The Gift, whatever that was?

"Hmmph," said the present Witchy Wanda. "I hadn't noticed that before. Still, I don't suppose it made any difference. The Gift never develops in males."

Jackson watched Double W lead the boy to the train station, stopping to buy an ice cream cone at a shop where the Laundromat now stood. She settled him happily slurping away at the melting cone on the viewing platform, then disappeared among the crowd of people arriving and departing. Jackson saw her step aboard the train, never looking back.

It wasn't until he finished the ice cream cone and the train disappeared from sight that the little boy realized he was alone. He began to cry, softly at first, then louder and louder until the sound brought the station manager out.

"What's your name, little man?" the station manager asked.

The boy's face was turned from Jackson, and he didn't hear the answer. Mesmerized, Jackson almost didn't see the current Double W raising her hand and pointing at him. "You're wasting your time," he said, turning from the scene.

"Thanks to my little toy, your earpiece cannot protect you," Double W said. "Only your mind is here, and I cast a spell on it, Jackson McKinney."

Jackson felt his brain go fuzzy. He fought inside to keep control, but his attempt to focus was like wading through pudding. "When you return to your body," Witchy Wanda told him, "you will follow the other children to my house, where you will gladly climb into my cauldron."

Gently, she took the globe from him. The next thing he knew, they were back where they had started in the tent. Witchy Wanda pocketed the ball, and the blackness faded to gloomy daylight that clearly outlined the entrance to the tent.

Jackson stumbled past the flap and into the harsh glare of the gym's overhead lights.

The rest of the day streamed by like a cloud drifting across the sky. Waiting for the special activities bus to take the class back to school, Jackson didn't hear Rodney's approach until he found himself spun around to face his nemesis.

"Time to settle up," Rodney said, his long arms and sharp elbows at the ready, like weapons.

"Whatever." Jackson couldn't concentrate on Rodney. He was thinking about how warm and comfortable it would be in the copper kettle.

"I'll throw in the attitude adjustment free of charge."

Jackson found himself flung on the ground, wondering dreamily if he should have brandished his pocket knife. He thought perhaps his lip was cut, but he felt pleasantly numb, watching with curiosity as his hearing aid bounced along as though it had decided to take a trip. He saw a gleeful Rodney smash the device with his heel. He also saw Mr. Campbell advancing.

Jackson couldn't quite hear what was happening, but it appeared that Rodney was in a lot of trouble. He didn't really care, allowing

Indira to help him onto the bus as though he were an invalid. Back at school, he didn't pay much attention to the nurse clucking over him as she dabbed at his lip with something that burned.

However, he began to care very much when both his parents showed up at school to collect him. They'd brought along one of his older hearing aids, so when they stopped at the principal's office, he could follow along as his father said at the very least Rodney and/or his family would be replacing Jackson's hearing aid and that Rodney and/or his family and/or the school system would be lucky if a lawsuit wasn't filed.

Jackson resisted his parents as they tried to lead him out of the building, telling them school was almost over and it was time to go to Dewey's Department Store.

He had no intention of going to Dewey's. He would head straight for that cozy copper pot.

Instead, he found himself in his bedroom, where his mother made him take off his shoes and lie down on the bed, instructing him to rest while she prepared him a nice bowl of butternut squash soup. As soon as he was left alone, Jackson sat up and stuffed his feet in his sneakers. He sneaked past the bedroom where Grandpa was napping. He tiptoed down the stairs and past the kitchen, where Jackson's parents were discussing whether to call Rodney's parents and/or send a formal letter.

Easing open the front door, Jackson escaped and headed for 42 Crab Apple St. He arrived just as Witchy Wanda was opening the door for the princess, fairy, cat and Indira. He tried to elbow past them, worried there wouldn't be room in the kettle for all of them.

Witchy Wanda smiled. "Welcome," she said.

The fairy threw herself at her hostess, hugging the witch around the waist. "I love you," she said. "You are so beautiful."

Witchy Wanda lurched at the unexpected embrace, patting the girl on the back and trying to pry away the little clutching hands. Jackson watched with interest as a ball dropped out of the witch's robe pocket. It bumpity-bumped along just as merrily as had Jackson's hearing aid, right into the street.

Witchy Wanda thrust the fairy from her and whirled to retrieve her treasure. Too late. Just then, Officer Kearns rolled by in his cruiser, smashing the globe to bits. He braked and jumped out of his car.

"Hey," he yelled, advancing toward the group. "Don't you kids know better than to play in the street?" Then he saw Witchy Wanda's expression and froze, not from a spell, but from the expression on her face. "Uh, that didn't belong to you, did it?"

"It did, indeed." Witchy Wanda's voice could freeze the fur on a polar bear.

Suddenly, Jackson realized he was himself again. He looked at his companions. They blinked like little owls, seeming confused about why they were standing in the doorway of 42 Crab Apple St.

While Officer Kearns tried to apologize to Witchy Wanda, Jackson assessed the situation. Double W must have used the ball to cast her spell on the girls, too, and when it broke, it released all of them.

Officer Kearns had been backing up the entire time he was talking, and now he was in his car and speeding away from Witchy Wanda's wrath. Jackson wanted to kick himself for not enlisting the police officer's help. Jackson's hearing aid would protect him now, but if Double W chanted another spell, the girls would be ensnared again.

"So," Double W said brightly. "You're here to take my candy order for next year?"

"I guess," said Indira, crinkling her nose in puzzlement.

"Come right in."

Jackson interrupted. "I figured you guys would be down at Dewey's Department Store."

"Why would we want to do that?" demanded Jasmine the princess.

"I heard something about the latest installment of that pony series." Actually, he had merely heard Mr. Dewey wondering when he would receive a new shipment, but the lure of the popular books was the only thing Jackson could think of that would chase his classmates from Double W's door.

"What's the title?" Indira wanted to know. "I haven't heard anything about a new release."

Jackson had just recently dusted the covers of *The Pony in the Pines* and *The Pony in the Poplars*, so he said, "Maybe *The Pony in*

111

the Peach Orchard." Maybe was a good word, guarding a sentence from being a flat-out lie.

The girls squealed and fled, abandoning an astonished Witchy Wanda.

Double W seemed momentarily off balance from having lost her victims. But she quickly resumed her cool cover. "So," she said, leaning against the frame of her door. "You live to fight another day, Jackson McKinney."

"Looks that way," Jackson said, taking one step back, then two, to prevent her from simply grabbing him and hauling him inside.

"Oh, don't be so skittish," Double W said, idly twirling a lock of red hair with her index finger. "Even though you've got the smell of sugar on you, you've been eating too many whole grains and vegetables to be appetizing. You'd have blended well with those sweet girls, though." She sighed. "Go home. Get a good night's sleep." She started to shut the door, then paused and grinned. "But you might keep one eye open."

The door closed.

Part Five: The Elixir of Longevity

Jackson didn't sleep at all. Or at least he didn't mean to. He climbed into bed and lay there with both eyes wide open, expecting a witch to fly through the window on a broom, though he'd never seen Witchy Wanda airborne.

His pocketknife rested under his pillow. Violence begat violence, his grandfather had said. But Jackson had to defend himself. He'd read that driving a stake in the heart was a permanent vampire solution, so a knife stab just might destroy a witch.

His theory wasn't tested that night. Despite his intention to remain vigilant, he found himself waking to the greeting of sunlight.

Leaping out of bed, he raced downstairs, astonishing his parents by asking for oatmeal and orange juice. It was Saturday morning, his mother reminded him. Saturday mornings she usually let him have frozen waffles and syrup as a once-a-week treat. But Jackson insisted on oatmeal, and not the kind out of packets, either. He wouldn't consume even one ingredient that might tempt Double W.

Returning to his room, Jackson made up his bed, retrieving the pocketknife from beneath his pillow and stowing it in his pants. He still wasn't sure that he could really stab a living creature. But there was no one else to stop Double W. On the way out, he grabbed the Indian head penny and stuck that in his pocket, too.

As he approached 42 Crab Apple St., Jackson saw Officer Kearns at the door, holding the fluffy cat from the police station in his arms. Double W noticed Jackson and winked at him, but Officer Kearns had his back turned to the street, his attention focused on Double W.

"I know this doesn't make up for, you know, it was an accident, I didn't mean to run over the ball–" His face turning red, Officer Kearns stopped talking and simply extended the cat, which growled.

"They're not particularly tasty," Double W said, making no move to take the cat.

Officer Kearns looked startled. "No, no, I'm not giving it to you for game meat. This is a pet."

"It's all very confusing," Double W said. "Didn't you bring me as a housewarming present a small animal of the same approximate size and tell me it was delicious with gravy?"

"That was a squirrel," Officer Kearns said. "And it was dead. And skinned."

Double W considered the cat, which glared at her. "Haven't I seen this animal before? Isn't it your mascot?"

Officer Kearns seemed embarrassed. "To tell you the truth, it doesn't seem too fond of me." As if to prove the point, the fluffy cat

114

chose that moment to try to escape, raking a claw along the officer's arm. "But you've got a way about you."

Double W smiled. "I do, don't I?" When she smiled, she looked so beautiful it was hard to believe she could be so dangerous.

But the fluffy cat wasn't fooled. When she reached for it, it fought with all the claws and teeth it possessed, scratching and shredding any fabric or fleshy bits of Officer Kearns available.

Double W took it from the officer, grabbing it by the scruff of the neck and shaking its head back and forth. Momentarily stunned, the fluffy cat suddenly found itself cradled in Double W's arms with limbs pinned and its mouth clamped shut against the crook of her elbow. Only the tail was free to go about its business, and it lashed back and forth in anger.

"At the station, we called the cat—"

She stopped him. "I shall name it Evelyn."

"But the cat's a male, ma'am."

"Your point?" From within the folds of Double W's robe, Evelyn tried to growl. Jackson could have told Officer Kearns that lots of famous men were named Evelyn. Mr. Campbell went on and on about some writer named Evelyn Waugh.

"Um, nothing." Officer Kearns suddenly seemed to realize that he was free of his burden. "Good day, then." He turned and saw Jackson, flushing when he realized Jackson was staring at his torn sleeve and scratches. "Won't the truant officer be interested to know you're out on the streets?"

"It's Saturday, sir." Jackson didn't even try asking Officer Kearns if he could speak to him privately. Officer Kearns seemed permanently hypnotized by Double W, the way some of the girls in his class mooned over Mr. Campbell. Jackson would have to tackle Double W all by himself.

A pickup truck rumbled by. "Expired inspection sticker!" Officer Kearns said, with the enthusiasm of a kid who just saw the circus coming to town. He hurried to his cruiser and took off.

Double W stepped back inside her house, followed by Jackson, who didn't wait to be invited. "I want to talk to you," he said.

"Talk away," she said, walking into the kitchen. With one hand, she reached into a cabinet. Setting a can of condensed milk on the counter, she opened a drawer and gestured at a handheld opener to Jackson. "Take care of that for me, will you?"

He should have stabbed her in the back while she walked from the front door to the kitchen. Now, he'd have to wait until she released the cat. It might not have the best personality, but he didn't want to hurt it. Jackson opened the can of milk. Double W rummaged in the cabinet for a bowl, poured in the milk and set the bowl on the floor.

When she relaxed her grip, Evelyn jumped from her arms, running past the bowl and out of the kitchen.

Now was his chance. Jackson fingered the knife in his pocket, but found he couldn't pull it out. "Would you really eat a cat?" he said, hoping that as he talked he could work up the nerve to do what needed to be done.

"Why not?"

"You're evil," Jackson blurted.

"I am no more evil than you, Jackson McKinney. I am a predator, as are you. You gobble hot dogs without even considering the animals whose lives were sacrificed."

"That's different." Just as Jackson's fingers closed around the knife, Evelyn came skulking back into the kitchen, burying his nose in the bowl of rich milk.

Double W laughed. "Everything must be true to its nature. Dear Evelyn follows the commands of his greedy nature."

Jackson whipped the knife out of his pocket. But his fingers fumbled, and it seemed to take forever to unfold the blade. With a snap the knife finally opened and he waved the blade at Double W. "Your murdering stops right here, right now."

"Go ahead," Double W said, not even trying to defend herself. "I don't think your nature will allow you to attack an unarmed woman."

Jackson took a step forward, his blade aiming right for her heart. But he couldn't bring himself to strike the blow.

Double W suddenly reached out and grabbed the knife from him. Jackson braced himself for her attack. Instead, she plunged the knife into her heart herself. Then she withdrew it – clean as a newly laundered sheet – closed it, and handed it back to Jackson. "You disappoint me," she said. "I thought you'd be more creative than this."

Evelyn, who had been lapping milk all through the drama, finished and began washing his face. Jackson made his way over to the cat as though he were going to pet him. At least he could snatch Evelyn and dash out of the house before Double W could make kitty cutlets.

But Evelyn did not want to be rescued. He snarled and swatted at Jackson and ran over to Double W, who scooped him up and held the now willing captive in her arms. "Men are so easily conquered," she said.

"Don't eat him," Jackson said, despising the begging tone in his voice.

"I wouldn't dream of eating him," Double W said. "At least not when better fare is available." He knew she meant children, and began backing up out of grabbing range.

"That's right, don't turn your back on me," Double W said. She let the cat drop from arms to the floor, as though already bored with him.

Jackson scooped up the cat and raced through the front door. If a knife couldn't kill a witch, what could?

Evelyn wriggled out of Jackson's arms and shot away. Maybe he'd return to the police station. Jackson ran down the sidewalk, running so fast that he didn't see Indira until he collided with her as

118

she crossed the street. The bundled towel she'd been carrying fell and a scrawny black-and-white cat tumbled out. Truly Awesome escaped before either Jackson or Indira could react.

"Oh, great," Indira said. "Thanks for ruining weeks of work." She turned away from him, staring in the direction of the escapee, then shrugged. "I'll just have to try again. So, what's up with you?"

"What are you talking about?" Jackson asked. "I don't have a pup."

Indira turned toward him. "I said, 'What's up with you?' You look like you've seen a ghost or a witch."

"If you only knew," Jackson muttered, embarrassed at having misheard her.

"Then go ahead and tell me."

"I can't."

"Why not?"

Because he didn't think Indira or anyone else would believe him. Because he was used to having to deal with his problems himself.

"I saw you coming out of that house. What's going on?" She plopped down on the curb. "Sit. Talk."

To his surprise, Jackson found himself sitting. "What were you doing with that cat?"

"I've been trying forever to catch it," Indira said. "I can't stand to see it starving. My parents won't let me have a pet, but I figure if I could show it to them, they'd have to let me keep it."

Jackson nodded. Maybe Indira was all right. But if Jackson found it first, that cat was his.

"What's up with Wanda Lovecraft? Does this have something to do with Mumps?"

Jackson took a deep breath and began telling his story. Indira didn't laugh. She didn't call him a liar. Instead, she listened intently. Finally, when he had finished, she said, "You've been trying to fight her all by yourself?"

"Who would believe such a crazy story?"

"I believe you."

"Yeah, well."

"Yeah, well, what?"

"Maybe that's because you don't exactly fit in, either."

"What do you mean? I fit in fine."

"Yeah, right," Jackson said. "You follow those girls, but you're not really part of their group." Right now, she didn't smell very good, either, but he didn't want to say that.

"Look," Indira said, "If this is about that hearing aid, get over it. Everybody's different in some way."

"Whatever." Jackson stood.

Indira jumped to her feet. Something dropped out of her pocket, and Jackson was relieved to discover the source of her foul odor was an empty tuna can in a sandwich bag. "We've got to get some adults to help."

Jackson shook his head. "Already tried talking to Officer Kearns."

120

"Of course he's not going to do anything," Indira said. "He's nutty about her. We could talk to Mr. Campbell."

"He won't listen, either," Jackson said.

"You might be surprised."

They were interrupted by the sounds of a feline yowl nearby. "Truly!" Jackson said.

"Snow Boots!"

The two looked at each other. "What kind of a name is Snow Boots?" Jackson wanted to know.

"What kind of name is Truly?" Another yowl, this one sounding like a cry of pain, sent them running back up the street.

They found Truly and Evelyn locked in combat in Double W's front yard, and it looked like Truly was getting the worst of it. Jackson and Indira ran onto the lawn, yelling and waving their hands. Startled, Evelyn loosened his toothy grip on Truly's leg. Truly took off, running with a limp. Evelyn pranced to the front door of 42 Crab Apple Street and meowed until the door opened just enough for him to slip inside. As the door closed, Jackson thought he saw a grin on the face of the shadowy figure of Double W.

"We've got to find Snow Boots," Indira said, moving down the sidewalk. "Who knows what kind of wound it got from that nasty cat?"

"I bet I know where Truly went to hide," Jackson said. He led the way to the depot, only to find Leon and Alonzo trying to coax Truly out of his hiding hole. Rodney, who apparently had nothing better to do than sit on the depot railing like a vulture, ridiculed the duo.

"You think that cat is going to come out for a piece of fruit leather?" Rodney laughed. Jackson wondered about the bruise on Rodney's face. He didn't think he'd struck even one blow when Rodney had jumped him, but maybe Jackson had gotten lucky.

"It's all we've got," Leon said.

"What are you guys doing?" Jackson asked.

"We've been trying to catch Patches for weeks," Alonzo said. "He's nearly starved to death."

"Patches?" Jackson asked.

"That's what we thought we'd name him."

Indira scooted closed to Truly's hideout. "Here, kitty, kitty," she crooned.

"Here, kitty, kitty," Rodney mocked. "What's that perfume you're wearing? Stinky No. 5?"

"Hey, that's a great idea," Indira said. She brought out the empty, but still highly aromatic, tuna can and set it on the ground. "Everybody back off."

They all scooted back, with the exception of Rodney, who remained on his perch. The cat's hunger overcame its fear and it crept forward. It limped a little, but it crammed its face in the can, licking up every last scrap and drop of juice.

Alonzo started forward. "Don't you dare," Indira said. "That's my cat."

"That cat's coming home with me," Leon said.

"What are you talking about?" Alonzo said. "You were just supposed to help me catch Patches."

"No, you were supposed to be helping *me*," Leon said.

Truly ignored them all, scooting the can along the ground in an attempt to extract the last possible morsel.

Rodney loomed over them, laughing. "This is rich," he said, "fighting over that scrawny thing." Truly removed his head from the can to track the source of the noise.

"Guys, I've got an idea," Jackson said. "Let the cat choose." He crouched and called softly, "Come here, Truly."

Indira immediately chimed in with, "Here, kitty, kitty." Truly stood and looked from one to the other.

Alonzo launched into a dramatic appeal. "Patches, I beseech thee to honor my humble home with thine presence."

"Pretty Patches, come play with me," sang Leon in his rich, velvety voice.

Jackson figured the cat would just run away from all of them. To his amazement, Truly limped over to him. Jackson gently picked up Truly.

"Even better," Rodney said. "One cripple picking another."

Jackson thought nothing could compare to the heat of Double W's cauldron, but the blood in his veins now seemed to be on fire. Of all the names he'd been called, no one had ever said the word *cripple*.

Before Jackson could react, Indira pointed to Rodney's face and said, "Looks to me like you've got your own problems."

Rodney's face flushed, and he slid down from the railing. Jackson tensed, and he saw Alonzo and Leon doing the same, wondering if they'd have to fight Rodney to protect Indira. But Indira stood steady, seeming perfectly capable of defending herself.

Rodney looked at the four of them, then said, "I got better things to do. Like go home and watch the grass grow."

"Go home and get beaten is more like it," Leon said after Rodney had walked away.

"What are you talking about?" Indira asked.

"When his dad gets mad, he takes it out on Rodney," Leon said. "I heard the same thing about Mumps's dad. Maybe Mumps really did run away." But Jackson was sure he hadn't.

"If so many people know about it, why doesn't anybody do anything?" Indira asked. "Somebody should report that man, make him take an anger management class. We could talk to Mr. Campbell, and maybe he could talk to social services–"

"Anger management class?" Alonzo asked. "Is that like detention?"

"Sometimes," Jackson told Indira, "you have to take care of things yourself."

"I'm talking to Mr. Campbell," Indira said. "You can't always handle everything alone, Jackson. Especially not what's going on at 42 Crab Apple Street."

Jackson could have kicked her for opening her big mouth.

"What are you talking about?" Alonzo asked. "What's going on at 42 Crab Apple Street?"

"Tell them," Indira urged.

"Tell us," Leon urged.

Alonzo struck a pose, hand on hand, warbling in a granny tone, "Now, sonny, *do tell*."

Jackson looked at the friendly faces of the guys, and at Indira's pleading expression. He told, softly stroking the little body he held in his arms.

"No way," Leon said after the tale had been told. "No offense, Jackson, but maybe Rodney rearranged your brains when he clobbered you."

"No, it makes sense," Alonzo said. "Think about it. Remember how weird everybody seemed at that Halloween party? Remember how dopey Indira and her pals acted when they came out of the fortune teller's tent at the carnival?"

"We didn't act *dopey*," Indira protested.

"Hypnotized, then," Alonzo said.

"Let's say you're right," Leon said, "and an evil force has infiltrated Glasglen. Now what?"

"We go to Mr. Campbell—" Indira began.

"Sure," Leon said before Jackson could protest. "Cranky Campbell's the one that sent us to her house on Halloween."

"But he didn't know—"

125

This time it was Alonzo who cut her off. "First," he said to Jackson, "you'd better go home and convince your folks to take Patches/Snow Boots/Truly to the vet." Jackson had seen this Alonzo before. This was the Alonzo who wanted to Direct as well as Act. "We all come up with a plan, then meet back here at 1200 hours to see who has the best strategy."

"What?" Indira asked.

"Noon."

"Can't we wait until after lunch?" Leon asked.

"You're the one that brought up evil infiltration," Alonzo said.

"Yeah, well, I think better on a full stomach," Leon said. "Let's say 1300 hours."

As expected, Jackson's parents said no way was he keeping a cat. Did he know how much cat food and litter cost? What about shots? But the cat was starving, Jackson said. *And* it was injured. That's what shelters are for, Jackson's father said. But nobody would adopt a crippled cat, Jackson said, nearly choking on the despised word. He wished Grandpa was there to back him up, but his grandfather was in his room, having one of those episodes where he'd just sit and wouldn't talk.

And then Truly, who always seemed so skittish before, started rubbing against the pants of Jackson's father and purring. The next thing Jackson knew, he was in the vet's office with his very own cat. The vet cleaned the bite wound, asking whether there was any chance the other cat had rabies.

"No," Jackson said. The way Officer Kearns was always quoting rules and regulations, Jackson was sure Evelyn was up to date on all the shots the vet had just given Truly. "It's just evil," Jackson added.

The vet smiled and said animals did not have the capacity for evil. The vet also said Truly might always have a slight limp from ligament damage, but otherwise, she was fine.

"She?" Jackson asked. And then he looked more closely. Sure enough, Truly was missing the standard equipment for males. It was bad enough he couldn't have a dog. Now he was stuck with a girl cat.

Truly, who did not care for the cold metal examining table, meowed so pitifully that Jackson automatically picked her up. She bumped the top of her head against Jackson's chin and started purring.

At 1300 hours, having left Truly in the cooing care of his mother, Jackson was back at the depot. So were Indira, Alonzo and Leon.

"You guys are going to love this," Alonzo said. "We'll stage a show in the school gym, and then when the lights go down, we'll nab her."

"Genius," Leon said. "Let's give her all the time in the world to gobble up the kids in town while we spend our time getting permission and working on a show."

"And what's your great plan?" Alonzo asked.

127

"I'm still digesting lunch," Leon said. "I can't think when my stomach's so full."

Jackson fumed. He should have handled the situation on his own. This was just a waste of time.

Indira spoke up. "Guys, I have a plan. First, we go talk to Mr. Campbell–"

"There's a surprise strategy," Alonzo said.

"I knew you were going to say that," Indira said. "What I'm suggesting is that we go and talk to him like this is a hypothetical situation."

"Hypowhat?" Leon asked.

"You know, pretend. That way, we can get his advice and then figure out what we need to do."

"And why do we want his advice?" Leon asked. "He sent us right into danger on Halloween."

"True," Indira agreed. "But he's an expert on ancient customs."

"How do you know?" Jackson asked.

"Because he's told us," Indira said. "More than once. He has what we don't – information."

"What do you think, Jackson?" Leon asked.

"What?" Jackson asked. He'd heard his name, but a passing car had muffled the first part of the sentence.

"I said, 'What do you think, son of Jack?' " This time, Jackson could hear the impatience as well as the sentence. People sometimes thought he wasn't paying attention when he didn't catch their words.

Jackson's plan had been to simply show up at 42 Crab Apple St. and try to poison Double W again, maybe having one of the other kids pretend to be selling something else from school. He wasn't crazy about the plan, because it meant putting someone else in danger, but he hadn't been able to think of anything else. Now he was thinking about when Grandpa had talked to him about knowing his enemy. Maybe telling the other kids had been a good idea, after all.

"I think Indira's right," Jackson said. "I think we need more information."

"Oh, great," Alonzo said. "We've got to track down a teacher on a Saturday."

Tracking down Mr. Campbell turned out to be the easy part. As they walked through the town, arguing about where he might be, they spotted him sitting by the window of the coffee shop, reading a book. Indira eagerly pulled open the door, followed by Alonzo and Leon. Jackson glanced down the street to Dewey's Department Store.

"Wait a minute," he said. "I know someone who knows Double W better than anybody."

Leon paused on the threshold. "Oh, yeah?"

"Hey, kid," hollered the woman at the counter. "Were you raised in a barn? Shut the door." Mr. Campbell looked up from his book and frowned, first at the woman, then at his students.

They hastily retreated back outside to the sidewalk. "If you're talking about that mannequin–" Indira began.

"She's not a mannequin, she's a person," Jackson interrupted.

129

Alonzo squinted down the street. "I dunno, she's doing a pretty good imitation of an inanimate object." He struck a pose, plunging one hand in his pocket and pretending to hold a pipe in the other. "Nothing to it, really."

"Except keeping your mouth shut," Leon said.

"Anyway," Indira said. "What could she know? She's been under a spell for years and years."

Jackson could predict a long argument. "Tell you what," he said. "You and Alonzo talk to Mr. Campbell, and Leon can go with me to the store."

As Jackson and Leon walked to Dewey's Department Store, Leon said, "So what's the plan?"

"Just go along with whatever I say."

"Uh huh," Leon said in a tone that suggested he was less than confident in Jackson's leadership ability. But he followed Jackson into the store.

Mr. Dewey, hunched over his cash register, looked up at the sound of the bell tinkling in the doorway. "McKinney," he said, "you know I close early on Saturdays. I was just finishing the day's accounting."

"Yes, sir," Jackson said to the old fraud. "But I've been thinking that front display would look a lot better if the platform was polished. Leon said he could help me move all the heavy stuff."

Mr. Dewey scrutinized Leon, who looked stunned. "Help, as in volunteer help? As in no payment-for-services-rendered help?"

"Yep," Jackson said.

"Stay right here," Mr. Dewey said. "I've got a wonderful cream polish that will make those pine boards shine."

Watching Mr. Dewey disappear behind the curtains, Leon said, "What kind of plan is that?"

Mr. Dewey emerged from the curtains with the polish, explaining that he'd set the bottom lock so that the boys could just close the door on their way out. He fretted about leaving the display window empty over the weekend, but he wanted the wood to soak up all the polish before replacing the furnishings. "Curiosity couldn't hurt sales," he finally decided.

As Mr. Dewey left, Jackson leapt onto the stage, shoving the suitcase at Leon. "Here, take this."

Leon staggered under the load. "Don't tell me you're really going to polish those boards," he said, setting the suitcase on the floor.

"Got to," Jackson said, pushing the rigid Miss Margot toward Leon.

"Why don't you just wake her up?"

"Not yet." Jackson never knew how long she'd stay awake, and he couldn't afford to waste time explaining why he needed to polish the floor.

Leon grunted at the weight of Miss Margot as Jackson sent her sliding from the stage. He had just settled her when Jackson scrambled off the platform with the display draping. "Here, help me fold this."

"Forget it," Leon said.

Jackson thrust a wad of fabric at him. "We've got to do the work in case Mr. Dewey walks by. We don't want him coming in here."

"What difference does it make?" Leon asked, but he began folding. He also helped Jackson polish the pine, though he did so while singing about how nobody knew the troubles he'd seen.

"OK," Jackson said when they were done. "Here we go." He fished the Indian head penny out of his pocket and tapped it against the display glass.

Miss Margot blinked and dropped her gaze down to her pin-striped overalls. "So it wasn't just some awful nightmare. This really is what I'm wearing." She yanked the red velvet cap off her head and threw it on the floor.

"Wow," Leon said.

Miss Margot started fluffing her hair with her fingers. "It's the latest style."

"Umm, I meant–"

"No time to talk," Jackson said. He grabbed Miss Margot by the hand and led her to the door. "Come on."

Miss Margot looked around. "Where is the proprietor? Where's my suitcase? And where's–"

Jackson yanked the door open and pulled Miss Margot with him. Leon followed, shutting the door behind them.

And just like that, Miss Margot walked into freedom. She stood on the sidewalk, taking deep breaths. "Chimney smoke. Wet leaves."

Indira and Alonzo burst out of the coffee shop, hurrying toward the store. "You won't believe what we found out," Indira said. Then she stopped as she and Alonzo recognized the woman who had been standing in the storefront their entire lives.

"Wow," Alonzo said.

Miss Margot flipped her hair and beamed. The fresh air seemed to have revitalized her. Jackson wondered if maybe she could stay real as long as she was outside.

Mr. Campbell came out of the coffee shop and began walking down the street toward them. "Oh, hello," he said in a tone Jackson had never heard.

"Hello," Miss Margot said in a voice that would make even honeybees gag.

"Beautiful day, isn't it?" Mr. Campbell asked, though, in fact it was overcast, cold and damp.

"We gotta go," Jackson said, taking Miss Margot by the hand, squeezing it hard to try to send her a message of urgency.

She winced, but seemed to really wake up. "Please excuse us," she said sweetly to Mr. Campbell. "The children and I have a matter to attend to."

"Perhaps I could be of assistance," said the alien now inhabiting the body of Mr. Campbell.

Jackson pulled at Miss Margot's hand, but she ignored him. "Perhaps you could," she said. "Would you happen to know where we might find elderberry and Echinacea growing in the wild?"

"An interesting question," Mr. Campbell said. "Might I ask for what purpose?"

"No, you may not," Miss Margot said, but her response didn't bother Mr. Campbell at all.

"Excuse my intrusiveness," he said, pointing to the hill rising behind the store. "The specimens you seek can be found in those woods."

"Thank you," Miss Margot said. "Come, children." And with a flip of her hair, she walked away, leaving Mr. Campbell to gape after her. Jackson, Indira, Alonzo and Leon followed her as she turned down the first alley, which ended at a drainage ditch.

"And now we go foraging," Miss Margot said, eying the hill.

"No way," Leon said. "There might be snakes up there."

"This is crazy," Indira said. "Mr. Campbell told us how people in ancient times got rid of witches, and it doesn't have anything to do with digging roots."

"And how much field experience does Mr. Campbell have?" asked Miss Margot.

"You can't fight a witch with a bunch of wildflowers," Leon said. "We need firepower."

Indira jumped in eagerly. "Mr. Campbell said fire–"

"Hold on," Jackson said. "I saw what happened when she ate wild carrots."

"Exactly," Miss Margot said. "Elderberry and Echinacea are powerful healing herbs."

"Which means they're poison to–"

"Exactly," Miss Margot said.

Indira looked at her suspiciously. "But Jackson said you're cousins."

"Did he?" Miss Margot responded.

"Why would you want to destroy your own cousin?" Indira asked.

"Payback," Leon said.

"Revenge," offered Alonzo.

"Exactly," Miss Margot said. "I'll blend the herbs with some sickeningly sweet beverage."

"And how do you plan on getting her to drink it?" Indira asked.

"I'll tell her that I'll trade her the elixir of longevity if she'll lift my spell."

"What's that?" Leon asked.

"A means of extending life," Miss Margot said.

"But she's – you know," Leon said.

"Even someone with The Gift can suffer from fatality," Miss Margot said.

"You mean she can die," Alonzo said.

"Correct."

"Does the elixir actually exist?" Jackson wanted to know.

"She thinks so," Miss Margot said.

"If you really want elderberry and Echinacea, you can just buy cough lozenges," Indira said, pointing to the drugstore. "My mom's the pharmacist there."

Miss Margot allowed the children to lead her back down the alley before she paused. "I'm just going to run back in the store for my suitcase."

"No, it's too dangerous," Jackson said.

"I want my suitcase," Miss Margot said. "It's mine." She stalked down the street to Dewey's door, the kids following her.

"It's locked," Leon reminded her.

"Not for long," Miss Margot replied. She pulled a bobby pin from her hair and within a few minutes had the door open.

"Don't go back in there," Jackson said. "What if you freeze again? I'll get the suitcase."

"Don't be ridiculous," Miss Margot said. "I'm fine now." She marched into the store, trailed by Leon.

Indira and Alonzo started to follow, but Jackson said, "You two stand watch." He walked into the store just in time to see Miss Margo bend to pick up the suitcase – and freeze.

Jackson reached in his pocket for the penny. It wasn't there. He jammed a hand in his other pocket. No penny.

"Hurry up," Leon said. "Do your little tapping routine."

"I lost the penny," Jackson said.

"Maybe you don't need the penny," Leon said. He dug into his pocket and handed over a quarter. Jackson tapped the code. No response.

"Now what?" Leon asked, plucking a business card from the sales counter.

"Now we go look for the penny," Jackson said. He thought about leaving the door ajar, but that might draw attention. He left the store, with Leon right behind him. When Jackson found the penny, he'd tap on the glass from the outside and Miss Margot could let them in herself.

But Jackson could not find the penny. Not even with Leon, Indira and Alonzo scouring the street and alley. "Time for Plan C," Alonzo announced.

Jackson wanted to shout in frustration. They'd left Miss Margot hunched over a suitcase. He'd lost the penny his grandfather had given him. Double W could be out prowling for another kid right now.

"What happened to Plan B?" Leon asked.

"There is no Plan B." Alonzo said. "I'm talking about Plan Campbell." He stuck out his arm as though presenting Indira. "Take it away."

Fire. Water. Air. Earth. Indira repeated what Mr. Campbell had said about some ancient people believing that the elements of nature must be combined in order to defeat evil.

"That's it?" Leon wanted to know. "That's the backup plan? It seems a little short on details."

"Well, he did say that some people used to believe that if you put a hair from a witch in a bottle and threw the bottle in a fire, that would kill the witch."

"It could work," Jackson said.

"How?" Leon asked.

"We tell Double W that Miss Margot wants to meet with her at the store. We tell her exactly what Miss Margot told us. She drinks the elixir."

"She turns to stone," Leon said.

"Right," Jackson said. "Then we drop the rock in the bottle and the next time my parents build a fire in the fireplace, goodbye forever."

"What if the bottle explodes?" Indira asked. "People could get hurt. And how are you going to get a hair from her head?"

"The stone must have her hair inside," Jackson reasoned. "And I'll figure out something about the fire."

"I'll go and tell her Miss Margot wishes to speak to her," Alonzo said.

"No, I'll go," Jackson said. "She can't cast a spell on me as long as I'm wearing my hearing aid. The rest of you get everything ready." Indira said her mother would let her have the lozenges and a soda. "Get something with as much high-fructose corn syrup as you can find," Jackson said. Leon said he could find an old canning jar in his grandmother's basement to use for the bottle.

"How are we going to get inside the store so we can hide?" Indira asked.

"You're not going inside the store," Jackson announced. "There's too much danger that Double W could cast a spell on you. Just meet me back here with the stuff."

Indira asked, "How are you planning to get back inside, anyway?"

"Uh oh," Jackson said. He was stumped.

"Not to worry," Leon said. He led them to Dewey's door. Looking closely, Jackson could see the tip of one of Mr. Dewey's ivory-colored business cards wedged between the lockset and the door frame. "Just a little insurance," Leon said.

Jackson hurried toward Crab Apple Street. He intended to just pop in at his house long enough to grab his backpack so he'd have some way of sneaking the jar in the house later. But his mother caught him and informed him that he could start right now being responsible for his pet. He found himself scooping out clumps from Truly's new plastic litter box. Gross. Then he had an idea for an excuse to leave the house. Calling to Truly, he coaxed her to climb into his backpack, which he then hoisted on his back.

When his mother asked him what he thought he was doing, Jackson said he was taking Truly out for some fresh air. Just as Jackson's mother began objecting, saying that she didn't think a cat, especially one that had just been injured, wanted to go bumping along in a backpack, Truly stuck her head out and began purring.

She stopped purring and starting wailing when Jackson paused outside his house to zipper the compartment shut. "It's just for a few minutes," he assured her, hurrying toward 42 Crab Apple St.

Answering his knock, with evil Evelyn in her arms, Double W said, "Oh, it's the Knife Wielder." Evelyn's growls were answered by Jackson's backpack. "I wonder," Double W said, stroking Evelyn's thick fur, "how long a cat can go without oxygen?"

Jackson hadn't thought of that. "I've got a message for you," he said. "Your cousin wants you to meet her at Mr. Dewey's store."

"That seems highly unlikely," Double W said. "since she's a mannequin."

Jackson shrugged. "She said something about an elixir of longevity. But you do whatever you want." When he saw the expression on Double W's face change, Jackson ran off, sure that the promise of immortality was enough to lure the enemy to the store.

Jackson stopped at the end of the next block to unzip the backpack just enough to give Truly some air, but not enough to give her a chance to jump out. He rushed back to the store, where Leon, Indira and Alonzo stood outside. They presented him with a Mason jar filled with a purple liquid. "Elderberry, Echinacea and grape drink," Alonzo said. "Yum."

"Thanks, guys," Jackson said. "Now leave."

"No way," Indira said.

Time was running out. Double W could arrive any minute. "Somebody's got to take care of Truly." He thrust the backpack at

Indira. "And someone's got to be ready to follow Double W in case she escapes." He pointed around the corner. "You can watch from there." He slipped inside the building and quickly repositioned Miss Margot so that she was standing.

Moments later, Double W entered the store and greeted Jackson. "Look at what I found on the way here," she said, rummaging in her robe pockets and producing a copper coin. "An Indian head penny. So it's my lucky day." She looked at the jar in Jackson's hand, then at the immobile Miss Margot. "You've set a little trap, it seems."

"She woke up long enough to tell me about the elixir of longevity," Jackson said, holding up the jar. "She wants to exchange it for her freedom."

"Why in the world should I think that's really the elixir?" Double W asked. "You drink first."

Jackson unscrewed the lid and tipped the jar. He couldn't taste the herbs for the sugary grape. He swallowed and replaced the lid.

"Aha," Double W said. "If it's palatable to you, then it must be poison to me."

He had to make himself sick, but how? Jackson thought about never finding the penny, about having to explain to his grandfather that he wasn't worthy of the trust placed in him. That made his stomach hurt, but it didn't nauseate him. He thought about the mess in Truly's litter box, but that wasn't enough. Then he imagined himself picking up the clumps and eating them. Suddenly, purple liquid spewed from his mouth. He bent over, hugging his gut with his free hand.

"Give me that jar," Double W said, snatching it from him.

Groaning, Jackson looked up just enough to see her removing the lid and sniffing at the contents. "Sweet elixir," she murmured. "Or trickery?" Then she looked beyond him and Jackson straightened, shifting his gaze to follow hers. She was staring at the clumps of grass on Miss Margot's boots. "So she's been outside. Perhaps it's true," she said. She set the jar on the sales counter and considered it. "Perhaps just one small taste–"

Just then the door tinkled and Rodney walked in. "Mom wants me to pick up–"

"Young Rodney, I cast a spell on you," Double W said before he could finish his sentence. She grabbed the inert boy and dragged him over to where Jackson stood. "Truth time, Jackson, if you care about your friend."

"He's not my friend," Jackson said. "I don't care what you do to him."

"You don't?" And just that quick, Double W had reached into Jackson's pocket and grabbed his pocketknife. She held the knife to Rodney's heart. "This is the tastiest of the organs," she said. She made her way to the counter, and picked up the jar. "If this poisons me, my hand will contract and this boy will die. Shall I drink it?"

If Jackson said yes, Rodney would die. Rodney was rotten, but Jackson didn't want to issue his death warrant. And yet, Rodney was only one person. If Double W didn't drink the potion, who knew how many children she might slaughter? What was one life worth?

"Don't drink it," Jackson found himself saying.

"I thought you didn't care about him." She set the jar back on the counter and pressed the knife harder against Rodney's chest. "You might want to close your eyes. This won't be pretty, especially not with such a pitiful tool."

"We made a deal!" Jackson protested.

"Check the fine print," Double W said. "By the way, I'm sure your little friends hiding around the corner will make nice filets, too."

"I don't know what you're talking about," Jackson said.

Indira, Jackson's backpack bouncing on her back, burst into the store, followed by Alonzo and Leon. "What's–"

That's when everything went crazy. Indira's jostling must have loosened the backpack zipper even more, because Truly suddenly flew through the air, landing on Double W's shoulder, snaring herself in that long red hair as she tried to keep from falling. Double W dropped the knife and Rodney as she flailed at her furry assailant, one arm knocking the jar off the counter, where it smashed onto the floor.

Double W slipped on the liquid and fell face first, her lips and nose bathed in the purple pool. Suddenly, she rolled over on her back, her eyes bulging, her ears reddening. Truly's back arched and her tail went on red alert as Double W began flickering and shrinking.

"Wow," Alonzo said when nothing but a heart-shaped black stone and a penny remained.

"Incredible," agreed Indira.

"We've got to get him out of here before he realizes what's going on," Jackson said, gesturing to Rodney, who was picking himself off the floor as though he'd just awakened him from a nap.

Alonzo hustled the groggy boy out the door. "Hey," Alonzo said, "I heard they got a new engine down at the fire station."

"Let go of me," Jackson heard Rodney say as the door closed. "Really?"

Time to rescue Miss Margot once again. Jackson picked up the penny and tapped it on a glass-topped display case. Nothing. Carefully, he pecked the code again. No response. Had Double W ruined the penny?

"We'd better get going," Indira said.

Miss Margot would have to wait. "Do you think," Jackson asked Leon, "your grandmother would give you another jar?"

"Sure," Leon said. "But the legend says you have to use a hair, not stone."

Indira, who had picked up Truly to soothe her, said, "Look."

The boys crowded around and Jackson plucked something from Truly's black-and-white coat.

It was a long red hair.

Part Six: Miss Margot's Revenge

An odd parade marched along the streets of Glasglen, led by Jackson, who carried an empty pack on his back and a lucky penny in his pocket. He was followed by Indira, bearing Truly Awesome in her arms. Leon carried a Mason jar, containing a red hair and a black stone, while Alonzo practiced the strutting posture of a warrior, a role he might play some day.

They paused when they reached 42 Crab Apple St. "Someone's going to have to go in first to see if Evil Evelyn's in there," Jackson said.

Alonzo flourished a pretend sword. "Stand back while I secure the way." Then he hesitated. "What if it's locked? What if she booby-trapped the place?"

"Only one way to find out," Leon encouraged him.

The warrior inched his way to the front door. He turned the knob and gingerly pushed. The door swung open, as Jackson knew it would. Double W had nothing to steal and no one to fear.

"Here, kitty, kitty," Alonzo called from the doorway.

145

"Go on in," Leon hollered.

Alonzo stepped just inside the doorway, then scurried back. "No evil kitties," he reported.

"Are you sure?" Indira asked, snuggling Truly.

"Let's do it," Leon said. "I gotta be home by suppertime."

They entered, easing the door shut again so that Truly couldn't run off. Even knowing that Double W could no longer hurt anyone, Jackson felt uncomfortable in her house, and he could tell the others did, too. He knew they all wondered what might have happened to Mumps here.

Jackson felt uneasy about bringing the other kids here. After seeing what almost happened to Rodney, he didn't want to take any chances with the others. When they'd cleaned up the mess at the store and stopped by the house of Leon's grandmother to get another container, Jackson had announced that he was taking the jar home and that he'd deal with the remains of Double W the next day, by himself.

That seemed to suit Alonzo and Leon just fine, but Indira had wanted to know how Jackson was going to dispose of the remains. When Jackson said he was going to build a fire in Double W's fireplace, then throw the jar with her hair and heart into the flames, she'd insisted they all go along, right then.

Now they stood in the chill of 42 Crab Apple St., looking at the empty fireplace yawning at them. Suddenly, the sound of a thump in the basement turned them all into statues as stony as Double W. Truly leapt from Indira's arms to hide in a corner. They all eyed the jar. If Witchy Wanda lay encased in glass, what lurked downstairs?

They heard feet treading heavily on the steps. It couldn't be Mumps, could it? And if it was, would he be some kind of monster now? Would it be better to try and run, or stay quiet and hope whatever it was would go back down into the basement? Jackson could see by the faces of the others that they had no idea what to do, either.

The basement door flung open to reveal Rodney. Everyone stared at each other. "What are you doing here?" Indira asked.

He glared at them. "None of your business."

"Were you looking for Mumps?"

"Yeah, well, maybe," Rodney said. "I dunno, I got this weird feeling today, and–" He shook his head as though to clear away a fog. "It's none of your business, anyway. What are you doing here?"

"We're–" began Indira, and Jackson knew she was going to tell him the truth because she didn't believe in hiding anything.

"–conducting an experiment," Alonzo interrupted.

"How come you have to do it here?" Rodney wanted to know.

"We need a big fireplace," Leon jumped in.

"And a jar," Rodney observed.

"And a jar," Alonzo agreed.

"Does anyone know how to build a fire?" Indira asked.

"I can do it," Jackson said. He squatted before the fireplace, grabbed a few skinny sticks of kindling lying on the hearth and began layering them among the logs. "Um, guys, I need matches." He stood. "Maybe I can find some in the kitchen."

"Chill, loser," Rodney said. Jackson wanted to shout at Rodney and shove him out the door, but he kept his mouth shut when he saw Rodney reach into his pocket and pull out a disposable lighter. Rodney also pulled out a pack of cigarettes, lit one and then tossed the lighter to Jackson.

All the kids gaped at the sight. Jackson couldn't believe Rodney was smoking and wondered where he'd gotten the pack and the lighter. Rodney coughed, then threw the cigarette down and ground it onto the floor, his eyes daring them to comment on his vandalism.

Jackson got to work with the lighter. Leon wasn't the only one who needed to be home by suppertime. If Jackson's parents had to come looking for him, he'd be in trouble the rest of his life.

The burning kindling ignited first one log, then another. Leon stood ready with the jar. "Now?" he said.

"No," Jackson said. "We'd better wait until it's really hot."

As the blaze grew, Truly crept from her corner to the door, and pawed at it. When it didn't open, she meowed, but no one answered her.

Indira looked at the window at the twilight sky. "The moon's already out," she said. "Can't we go ahead? I'll get into trouble if I'm not home by dark."

The flames were burning steadily now. "OK," Jackson said.

"Wait," Indira said, and ran to the door where Truly stood.

"What are you doing?" Alonzo asked.

"If that bottle explodes, glass is going to fly everywhere," Indira said. Alonzo sidled over to her, followed by a sheepish Jackson.

Rodney stood his ground. "Babies," he said.

Leon gulped, threw the bottle and ran to join the group at the door. Rodney strolled over to Jackson. "Give me back my lighter."

At first nothing happened. "Is there a plan D?" Leon asked.

Then came a pop from the fireplace. The lid, still attached to a jagged portion of the jar's neck, rocketed through the room, coming to rest on the spot where Rodney had stood. A little black stone streaked through the air, landing on the floor as though it had been spit out by the fireplace. Shards of glass sprinkled the hearth.

"Wow," Leon said.

The commotion made Truly paw frantically at the door. Indira picked her up and tried to soothe her.

"So that's it?" Rodney asked. "That's the big experiment?"

"Um, yeah," Alonzo said. "We wanted to see whether the glass would melt or break."

Rodney shook his head in disgust, yanked the door open and left.

"Are we done?" Indira asked, looking through the open door. "It's starting to get dark."

"I guess," Jackson said. "You guys go ahead. I'll just make sure the fire goes out." He intended to toss the stone back into the flames and watch to make sure the heart really would burn to ashes. As he began to walk toward the stone, it started to glow, probably from the

149

fire. But it hadn't been glowing before. Then Jackson perceived the weak moonlight illuminating the room. "No," he yelled, diving for the heart.

He landed on the floor and grabbed the stone, which had begun to vibrate, then dropped it as it seared his hand. He grabbed it again, but too late to stop it from transforming into a cloud of swirling, sparking black bits that began shaping into a woman. Jackson blinked and found himself holding the foot of Double W. He let go with a yelp and scooted back.

Double W grabbed her head with her hands. "Tell me it was a good party," she said.

Jackson edged away from her, stood and ran out the door, right behind Alonzo, Leon and Indira, still clutching a protesting Truly.

They paused at the end of the block to catch their breath. "Now what?" Leon demanded.

"Now we all go home," Jackson said.

"We just go home?" Indira asked.

"The transformation weakens her," Jackson explained, reaching for Truly. "We can regroup tomorrow."

"How about 0900 hours?" Alonzo asked.

"Tomorrow's Sunday," Leon said. "I've got a solo with the choir."

They agreed to meet at 0200 hours, because Leon said he couldn't miss Sunday lunch with his grandmother. He especially couldn't miss her butterscotch pie.

"Better take a pass," Jackson advised him. "Double W has a big sweet tooth. Eat your vegetables."

Jackson trudged home. Things were worse than ever. He'd had one chance to spring Miss Margot on Double W as a surprise, and he'd blown it. Even if he could bring Miss Margot back to life again with the penny, he couldn't see how she could help. Double W wouldn't fall for the elixir trick a second time. And now he'd exposed his friends. When Double W grew hungry again, first she'd go looking for the kids who knew her real identity. And those kids were now his friends.

Back at home, Jackson dutifully refilled Truly's water bowl and set out some dry cat food for her. She crunched in happy oblivion. Jackson didn't want any supper, but he commanded himself to shovel in extra helpings of asparagus and buckwheat noodles. He had to make himself as witch proof as possible.

Grandpa seemed more himself, and after supper, Jackson followed his grandfather to his room.

"Something on your mind?" Grandpa set aside his walker and settled himself in his armchair, his blue eyes shining, his face alert.

Jackson sat on the floor, his arms wrapped around his knees. "I've got a problem and I don't know what to do about it."

"Care to tell me about it?' Grandpa's face looked so kindly that it was hard to resist the temptation to tell him everything. But Jackson didn't want to get Grandpa into trouble. He'd already overheard his parents talking about whether they ought to consider a facility when

151

Grandpa had been having a really bad spell. Jackson couldn't risk him starting to talk about witches.

"I need to figure it out by myself," Jackson said. "Just like you had to figure out how to fight the enemy. What was it like shooting somebody? Did it help having somebody telling you what you should do?"

Grandpa ran a hand through his long white hair. "Jackson, I never shot anybody."

"You didn't?" Jackson unwrapped his arms and sat back.

"I never wanted to harm anybody. Not many of the boys did. I was fortunate in that I got to be a medic."

"So you saved lives instead."

Grandpa shook his head. "Not always. By choosing who got treated first, I had to let some people die. I think about that a lot."

Jackson let that sink in. "How did you choose?"

"You use your resources where it will make a difference."

"That makes sense," Jackson said.

Grandpa frowned. "Things were never that clear cut. I'm going to tell you something I've never told anyone else."

Jackson leaned forward, his heart pounding.

"I tended to another soldier while my best friend was dying."

Jackson said nothing. He couldn't imagine doing such a thing.

"My friend wasn't going to make it. So I treated the other injured man and gave my friend something to take away the pain."

"I guess that was the worst time of your life."

Grandpa considered Jackson with those clear blue eyes. "No, as bad as that was, my worst days occurred when I was much younger than you."

"What happened?"

Grandpa's face looked pinched, as though an old pain stirred inside. He fussed with his walker, shifting it to the other side of his chair. Finally, he spoke. "I'm an orphan," Grandpa said. "I was abandoned as a child and left in the care of strangers."

Jackson digested this information in silence. He hadn't really thought about it before, but most of his relatives were on his mother's side of the family.

"At first I wouldn't eat, and the people at the home had to force food down me," Grandpa said. "But then one day a little girl gave me her sock monkey to hold, and she sat and held my hand." Now Grandpa smiled a little. "That little girl grew up to be your grandmother."

"So did you ever find out what happened to your family?" Jackson asked. "And how come I never knew about this?"

"It was so long ago, and I don't remember all of it," Grandpa said. "I have a vague memory of coming to Glasglen on a train with two women. Then I remember being at the train station again with one of them. She got on the train and left me alone, a little boy who couldn't even speak a whole sentence. I never saw either of them again." The slight smile had disappeared.

Jackson had to make himself breathe. His grandfather was the little boy Jackson had seen in the vision in the tent. That meant ... No way. No way was Jackson related to that evil creature that lived at 42 Crab Apple St. No way was Double W his cousin.

Leaving his grandfather's room and stumbling to his own, Jackson flung himself on his bed, nearly jumping back onto to the floor when he heard a screech. Truly scrambled from her hiding place under the bed. When she determined the room was safe, she gave Jackson a look to make sure he knew she was offended, then proceeded to wash a paw.

Jackson stretched out on the bed and stared at the ceiling. It made sense, now, why only Grandpa's penny could make Miss Margot return to herself. It was the same penny that had first awakened her from Double W's spell.

If Double W really was his cousin, could he bring himself to destroy her? He had to. She was evil, and as soon as she recovered, she'd be looking for another kid to stew.

He meant to spend the night concocting the perfect plan for disposing of Double W, but his fatigued body won out. When his eyes opened again, the sun already was casting a spotlight that had been claimed by Truly, who lay on the floor with her tail curled almost to her nose. He looked at the clock beside his bed. Too late to sneak over to Double W's house before church.

Entering the church, he saw with dismay that his folks were headed for the pew in front of Rodney and his parents. Jackson had never seen Rodney's father in church. The man told Rodney to get rid of his gum, the voice starting out loud and angry, then dropping, like he was trying to change gears from fast to slow. Maybe Indira had talked to an adult and the telling had made a difference.

Jackson patted his pocket. Along with the penny and pocketknife lay a pack of gum that his own mom said he could have right after the service. It was sugar-free and contained ingredients like beeswax, but still, it was gum.

Jackson fidgeted on the bench between his parents and grandfather, wondering what Rodney had in store for him and wondering what Double W might be doing. He looked at his grandfather's face, but could see no resemblance to Double W. Maybe she'd been lying about the little boy's mother being her cousin.

Jackson tried to turn his attention back to the sermon, because he knew his parents would quiz him at lunch. The church was in between pastors, so every week meant another tryout. This process left Jackson very confused. One week he'd crept out of the church after being shouted at for an hour, feeling lucky not to be struck by divine lightning because the entire congregation was nothing but a bunch of worthless worms. Another week he was told he was a precious lamb.

The minister today was a woman talking about faith, hope and charity. He'd heard the verses before at a wedding, but the bride and groom had used the word love instead of charity. The minister's voice was calm and compelling. She explained the verses in a way that made sense to him. When she talked about seeing through a glass darkly, Jackson realized that was exactly how he felt about the Double W situation, about Rodney, about everything. He couldn't see all the angles in a situation, and he couldn't figure out exactly what he should do. Charity, the minister suggested, could be his guide.

As good a speaker as the minister was, still it was hard sitting for so long. Jackson shifted his weight. When he moved his feet, one shoe made a huge sucking noise as it tried to separate from a giant wad of gum. *Rodney.* The minister frowned in Jackson's direction, her sense of direction aided by the glares Jackson's parents directed at him. Grandpa didn't even seem to notice.

Jackson's shoe sighed as he tried to settle it back to the floor. The minister continued, but Jackson tuned out. How could you apply charity to Rodney? Defense and offense seemed to be the only words that applied to bullies.

After the service, Jackson's mother produced a nail file from her purse and proceeded to scrape away the gum with grim determination. Jackson knew he was in for another sermon later.

As the congregation filed out to be greeted by the minister, who stood at the door, Jackson had a suspicion that Rodney was waiting outside for him. With dread, Jackson waited while his parents chatted with the minister. He noticed that Grandpa seemed to be agitated. Leaning on his walker, he swiveled first to one side and then another. He sniffed the air.

"Fire!" Grandpa hollered. "Evacuate the premises!"

The congregation members, some still standing in line, some visiting, stopped and whipped their heads around, eyeballs rolling. "Fire!" "Where?" "Fire!"

Jackson's father yelled that it was all a mistake, but several people rushed around the church, grabbing hymnals and the altar flowers. Jackson's father yelled again there was no fire. When no smoke appeared, it finally was agreed that there was no fire and Jackson's parents hustled Grandpa into their car.

"Nice work," Rodney said as Jackson walked by to follow his parents. "Ask him to call in a bomb scare next week."

Jackson stopped. He wanted to hit Rodney, but that would not improve Jackson's health or his standing with his parents. He tried to think of some insult that would make Rodney feel like a worthless worm, but his brain wouldn't cooperate. Then, to his horror, he found himself reaching into his pocket and extending the packet of gum to Rodney. "Here," he said.

Rodney's long arm had begun to reach for the offering when he stopped. "Why would you want to give me anything?" he asked.

"Because you lost yours," Jackson said, shoving the gum onto Rodney's palm and then climbing into this parents' car. Maybe confusing the enemy scored almost as many points as defeating him.

At home, Jackson shoveled in brown rice and steamed snow peas as fast as he could. Grandpa seemed all right now, but he ate quietly. Jackson's parents didn't talk much, either. As Jackson made his way to the door, Truly followed, meowing. "Sorry," Jackson said. "I'll be back soon." He hoped that was a promise he could keep.

Approaching 42 Crab Apple St., Jackson stopped when he saw a patrol car parked on the street across from the house. He started to turn away when he noticed that Officer Kearns just sat there with Evil Evelyn in his arms, his hand repeatedly stroking the cat's back. Something was wrong. Officer Kearns wouldn't take a cat with him on patrol. A spell was at work.

Jackson had exactly half an hour before the other kids showed up. Now that he had gotten used to having backup, it seemed even scarier to go in there by himself. But he had to protect his buddies. And his urge to pay back Double W for what she had done to Grandpa overwhelmed his fear.

He sneaked around to the back of the house and peeked through the window. What he saw chilled him more than the cool November air. Double W stood at the fireplace, singing and pouring water in her kettle. Lying on the floor in a neat row were Indira, Alonzo and Leon. They seemed to be sleeping.

Double W walked from the great room to the kitchen. Maybe she'd spend a few minutes in there gathering her spices. Immediately, Jackson eased the window open and crawled inside. He bent over Leon and shook him to wake him up. Leon didn't stir. Jackson prodded Alonzo and Indira without success, either.

"I suppose you're here to save your friends." Double W walked in with a pepper mill. "Funny, that's what they thought they were going to do for you."

"You tricked them somehow," Jackson said, hoping to keep her talking while he tried to think of some way to rescue the sleepers.

"With the help of that darling Officer Kearns," Double W said. "He stopped by with Evelyn." She ground some pepper into the pot. "I can't imagine why Evelyn ran back to the police station." She ground some more. "Anyway, he was very willing to go to your friends' homes and ask if they'd seen you."

"That was dumb," Jackson said. "If they think a kid's missing, all those parents will call my parents. And they'll come looking for me."

"Oh, I doubt they'll want anything to do with you or your parents, not after Officer Kearns said he was looking for you to discuss the theft of property from my domicile." Double W stirred the contents of the cauldron. "But it certainly enticed your little friends to come running." She looked at the sleeping figures. "It was too easy, really. You're much more challenging. And entertaining."

Jackson knew he could save himself just by running out the door. But those kids wouldn't be stretched out senseless if he hadn't gotten them involved. It occurred to him that if Double W had something else to digest, the others might wake up in time to escape. Slowly, he raised a hand to his ear. Withdrawing the hearing aid, he carefully set it on the floor.

"Come and get me," Jackson said.

Double W smiled, then flared liked a star going nova. Her red hair seemed to crackle with electricity and her black eyes burned like smoking coals. "Jackson McKinney," she said in a voice rich with satisfaction, "I cast a spell on you."

Jackson felt his brain fogging and his body draining of energy. He thought he could go to sleep standing on his feet. Then the fog seemed to clear a bit and he wondered why he had ever thought the woman before him was scary. A golden glow lit her figure and her hair floated like an angelic nimbus.

"Why don't you step into this nice warm bath?" She gestured to the pot. "You smell like vegetables, but I'm too hungry to be picky."

"Sure, cousin Wanda," Jackson said, starting to move forward, but she stopped him.

"What did you call me?" The golden shimmer dimmed a bit. "I'm no relation of yours."

"Cousin," Jackson insisted, beaming at her. "My grandpa's the little boy you bought the ice cream for."

"This is growing tiresome," she said, snapping her fingers.

The golden glow vanished and Jackson once more found himself confronting the more familiar form of Double W. A slight stirring caught his eye. Maybe Double W had gotten so distracted over this relative business that she had broken the spells on his friends when she snapped her fingers. "So I'm Miss Margot's cousin, too," he said, trying to distract her further.

160

"No, not Margot. Another fabrication concocted for the benefit of Martin Dewey. Margot was my apprentice, and a poor one at that." Without his hearing aid, Jackson had to carefully watch her lips to make sure he understood what she was saying. "She had the potential of greed, but she was too tender-hearted."

"So was my great-grandmother really your cousin?"

"Yes, yes," Double W said, her voice sounding impatient. "And no, she did not have the Gift. Just a poor creature who did not survive childbirth. And yes, her husband really did die in a war." She gestured to the pot. "You're straying from the task at hand. You were just about to sacrifice yourself."

"Don't do it!" This came not from Double W, but from Indira, who slowly sat up. Leon and Alonzo were sitting up now, too, looking around as though they'd awakened from a nap.

Double W frowned and raised her arm. "Talk, not walk," she said. "And remember it would behoove you not to bore me." Jackson took the opportunity of her distraction to scoop up his hearing aid and slip it into his ear.

Indira ignored Double W's command and attempted to rise, but flopped back on the floor like a fish dumped on a pier. She rolled over and tried unsuccessfully to push herself onto her knees. "Let us go and I can bring you the real elixir," she said with one cheek on the floor, "My mom's a pharmacist."

Jackson quietly checked his pockets while his friends played with Double W's riddle. All he found were the Indian head penny and the

161

pocketknife. He wondered if he should try shoving Double W into her own fire. But if she grabbed him first, then there'd be no hope for the others.

"That's convenient," Double W said.

"It's the truth." Indira spoke to the ceiling, having rolled onto her back.

Double W considered the proposal. "But I'm hungry now."

"I got you covered," Leon said, struggling to dig into his pants pockets with his legs still glued to the floor. He tossed her a candy bar, apparently having ignored Jackson's advice about sweets. "Let me go home, and there's more where that came from."

Greedily tearing away the wrapper, Double W shoved the candy bar in her mouth, chewed it a couple of times and gulped it down. "A nice serving of saturated fats," she said. "But I'm still hungry."

"You want saturated, try the diner," Leon said. "They fry their hamburgers in bacon grease and then they pile the bacon on top. With cheese. But the fried chicken is the best."

"It's not the same as fresh flesh, but it might suffice as an appetizer." Double W strode to the door, opened it and pointed her finger in the direction of the patrol car. When the motor started and the car pulled away, she turned back to Jackson and the trio still flopping and wriggling on the floor. "While I await my delivery order, tell me what you can offer me as a guarantee that you'll return? Perhaps you might leave something of value."

Jackson offered her his pocketknife. Double W shook her head. Reluctantly, Jackson brought out the Indian head penny. She shook her head again. "You must leave something you really care about it. Bring me that creature you call Truly Awesome."

"No way!" Jackson said.

"Don't do it, Jackson," Alonzo said, trying to use his hands to raise his legs.

"We didn't give you that cat to let her make a kitty cake," Leon said.

"Hey, you didn't give me Truly. She picked me."

Double W pointed at the three bound to the floor. "Back to sleep." Immediately, they ceased struggling and closed their eyes. She turned to Jackson. "Make up your mind, now."

Hoping that she wouldn't proceed with her soup making, Jackson raced home, grabbing his backpack and telling his parents he was taking Truly out for some fresh air. She seemed to enjoy the ride, with her head poked out and taking in the passing scenery. But when Jackson started to go back inside 42 Crab Apple St., she started growling.

"Don't worry," Jackson said. "I won't let anybody hurt you."

He stepped inside and shut the door to find Double W cramming a dripping cheeseburger into her mouth. Evelyn tore into a piece of fried chicken. He looked up at the commotion, saw Truly and growled. Truly jumped from the backpack, landing awkwardly on her weak leg.

163

Evelyn abandoned the chicken and began padding toward Truly, who tried to limp away.

"Do something about your cat or the deal's off," Jackson said, scooping up Truly and cradling her in his arms.

Double W bent and murmured something in Evelyn's ear. His ears flattened, then he turned away, picked up a piece of chicken in his mouth and retreated to the kitchen. Double W returned to her cauldron. "I hope she's a good mouser. Evelyn's an excellent hunter." She dipped a ladle into the soup and brought out a gray lump with a tail. "Adds a little flavoring," she said, dropping it back into the kettle.

"How do I know you won't let your cat hurt Truly?" Jackson asked.

"Evelyn and I have come to an understanding," Double W said. "In negotiations, McKinney, trust is required."

Gently, Jackson set Truly on the floor. She trotted over to the remains of the fried chicken and began helping herself. Double W laughed. "A willing hostage, it seems."

"Indira's mom won't open the pharmacy until tomorrow morning," Jackson said. "I'll be back after school with the elixir." Pointing to his friends, he said, "Wake them up."

The four stood on the sidewalk outside 42 Crab Apple St.

"Now what?" Alonzo asked.

"Now we go check on Miss Margot," Jackson answered. He wasn't ready to tell the others that Double W might be his cousin, but he had to talk to Miss Margot. With the store being closed on a Sunday afternoon, and the business card still wedged beside the lock, they should be able to slip in without Mr. Dewey knowing anything about it.

That part went just fine. Then Jackson pecked the code on one of the glass-topped display cases. Nothing. Not a twitch or a blink from Miss Margot.

"Maybe you're sending the wrong message," Leon suggested.

Jackson carefully tapped the code. Nothing.

"Let me try," Leon said. "I know the rhythm." Jackson handed over the penny, but Leon had no better luck.

"Maybe it's got to be her display window," Indira suggested.

Jackson moved over to the window, though pecking on the case had worked just fine before. Again, he tapped the code. Nothing. No fluttering of eyelashes.

Staring at the coin in his palm, Jackson said, "Maybe Double W did something to it while she had it." After all, she'd seen his grandfather work magic with it in the vision in the tent. "Maybe she took away its magic." He would never know what Miss Margot could tell him about his family.

"How are you going to get your mom to make an elixir?" Leon asked Indira.

"She's not going to make it," Indira said. "I am. I just need to get some of those elderberry and Echinacea lozenges from Mom. I have no intention of giving Wanda Lovecraft a real elixir."

"She won't buy the old grape-drink scam again," Alonzo said.

"I have a better idea," Indira said. "My mom's always giving me perfume samples. I'm going to mix them all up. The stinkier the potion, the better Wanda Lovecraft will like it."

As the four agreed to meet Jackson at Dewey's Department Store after school, Alonzo posed a question. "And just how are we going to get her to believe this is the real stuff this time?" This had been worrying Jackson, too.

"We'll cross that creek when we get there," Leon said. "That's what my grandma always says." He dug into his pocket. "I wish I hadn't given that witch my candy bar." He kept digging, finally producing a gum ball and popping it in his mouth.

Jackson wished he hadn't given the witch his cat.

Sunday evenings were supposed to be reading evenings in the McKinney household. Jackson's father and grandfather, who seemed fine after the morning's episode, shared the newspaper, while Jackson's mother worked a crossword puzzle. Jackson tried to read one of his textbooks, but he couldn't concentrate, wondering if Truly was all right.

He looked over at Grandpa. Jackson wanted to tell him everything he'd discovered, but he'd already decided he'd better not. Jackson stared at Grandpa's wrinkled hands, the skin almost paper thin, the veins bulging. Years ago, those hands, though much smaller then, had worked one act of magic, stirring a spellbound Miss Margot to life. He wished Grandpa could work that magic again. Suddenly, Jackson set aside his textbook. What if ...

Walking over to his grandfather, Jackson said, "Grandpa, would you hold my penny for me?"

Jackson's mother looked up from her crossword puzzle and asked him why in the world did Grandpa need to hold his penny and why wasn't it in the display case in his room, anyway? Jackson said he'd brought it down from his room (which he had, though many days ago) so that Grandpa could make it lucky again (which was recently true).

Grandpa held out his hand for the coin. "Whatever luck I've got, I'll be glad to share it with you."

Jackson dropped the penny in Grandpa's palm and curled his fingers over the image of the wreath. Covering Grandpa's closed hand with his own, Jackson shut his eyes and squeezed, willing the magic of the little boy to work one more time. But as hard as he wished, he couldn't feel any magic.

When he opened his eyes, he saw his parents smiling at each other in amusement. Jackson didn't care. Because when Grandpa uncurled his fingers, Jackson saw the Indian's face – somehow, the coin had flipped in that tightly closed hand.

167

Minutes and hours had never gone by as slowly as they did the next day at school. Jackson hoped his parents, who were already used to Truly spending a lot of time in his room, would continue not to notice that Truly was missing. He'd rinsed out her water bowl and scooped a few bits of her kibble into his pocket to make it look she'd been nibbling. He'd even pantomimed cleaning her litter box.

Finally, Jackson found himself mopping in Dewey's Department store, trying to work out how, with Mr. Dewey right there, he could use his newly magicked penny to free Miss Margot. He'd decided he needed to arrive at Double W's before the other kids. He was sure the new potion scheme would fail and that Double W would stuff them all in her kettle. But if he could show up with Miss Margot alive, the element of surprise could help him rescue Truly. The only problem was how to distract Mr. Dewey so that he could sneak Miss Margot out. He didn't know how he'd explain a missing mannequin, but he could worry about that later – if there was a later.

Now the minutes were going by too fast as he kept working under the watchful eye of Mr. Dewey. Jackson had to come up with a plan before his friends could arrive. But Mr. Dewey kept staring straight at him. Or was he staring at Miss Margot, still parked off stage beside her suitcase?

"Festive flowers," Mr. Dewey said.

168

"Excuse me?" Jackson said, pausing so he could look at Mr. Dewey.

"I'm rethinking the entire display window," Mr. Dewey said. "I'm going to invite the florist to design an arrangement, highlighting some of my goods, for every season. Free advertising for her, free display design for me."

Jackson wondered why Mr. Dewey even bothered trying to earn real income, but maybe it was all part of his plan to retire rich without anyone suspecting. "That's a great idea," Jackson said. "My mom loves flowers."

Mr. Dewey beamed.

"Since you're going to change the window, anyway, could I borrow her for a school project?" Jackson indicated Miss Margot.

Now Mr. Dewey frowned. "What kind of project?"

"It's for cultures studies," Jackson said. It was all kind of true, if learning more about Double W could keep kids off her menu.

But Mr. Dewy seemed dubious. "And how do you propose to transport her to your school?"

That had him stumped. Just then the bell on the door jangled and his comrades trooped in, Indira's backpack bulging with the shape of a bottle. "They can help me carry the mannequin," he said, willing them with his eyes to go along.

"Sure," said Alonzo, who knew all about accommodating script changes. "We'd be glad to help you carry the mannequin."

And so Jackson, Alonzo, Leon and Indira strolled right out of the store, toting Miss Margot like a surfboard. As soon as they were outside, they propped her against the storefront.

"What's up?" Leon asked.

"Just watch," Jackson said. He peeked inside the window. Mr. Dewey's back was turned while he folded cashmere scarves. Quickly, Jackson took the penny out of his pocket and tapped it lightly against the glass with the code, hoping it wouldn't attract Mr. Dewey's attention.

The eyelashes fluttered. The blue eyes blinked. A hand lifted a stray hair from a cheek. Miraculously free once again, Miss Margot said, "Where's my suitcase?"

"Forget the suitcase," Jackson said. "We need your help."

Jackson practically pushed her down the street before Mr. Dewey could look up, but even as she walked, Miss Margot argued that any help she could provide would be enhanced with a ready supply of cash. Leon pointed out that her attachment to that money almost ended in her becoming permanent plastic.

"You don't understand," Miss Margot said. "I need that money for my search." And suddenly Jackson realized it was Miss Margot who really didn't understand, at least not the passing of time. She wanted to find that little boy.

Indira said it wouldn't be right to use the money, anyway, because now they knew it was counterfeit. Miss Margot stopped and asked how she could know it was fake unless she'd been helping herself, which made Indira puff up like Truly confronting Evelyn. "We don't need her help," Indira told the boys. "We can stop Wanda Lovecraft ourselves."

"Wanda Lovecraft?" Miss Margot said. "Why are we wasting time? Lead the way."

"How come you can't do some hoo-doo yourself and fix everything?" Leon asked.

Miss Margot looked grim. "I'm just a beginner. But I may have a talent for revenge."

Alonzo, Leon and Indira peppered her with questions as they walked, but she swatted them aside. "Just take me to her house."

When they arrived at 42 Crab Apple St., Miss Margot marched right in, not even bothering to knock.

"Maybe you guys better wait outside," Jackson said. "Double W could cast another spell on you."

"And miss this scene?" Alonzo said. "No way." He and the others pushed through the door, followed by Jackson.

They found Double W at her kettle. Truly lay in one corner washing a paw while Evelyn glowered at her from another corner. "Oh, hello, Margot," Double W said to the intruder.

"Oh, hello, Margot? That's all you have to say after locking me up for decades?" Jackson thought Miss Margot might be capable of going nova without the help of magic. He and his friends stood silently to see what would happen next.

"Would you like some soup?" Double W asked. "Truly and Evelyn brought me two choice morsels just this morning."

"No, I don't want any of your hideous soup," Miss Margot said.

"That's why your gift never grew," Double W said. "You didn't feed it properly."

Jackson could almost feel Indira's agitation. "You're a criminal and a monster," she burst out.

Anticipating Double W's anger, Jackson edged away, prepared to make a grab for Truly and dash out the door, hoping the others would make a run for it, too.

But Double W merely responded, "I make no apologizes for who I am, Indira, eater of fish, Leon, gnasher of cows, Alonzo, chewer of pork products. As for you, Margot," she said, "Be content that I spared your life, whatever shape it has taken." Now she smiled.

"You didn't spare me. You robbed me of my life." Miss Margot advanced on Double W. "What did you do to that poor little–"

"Spare me the theatrics," Double W said. "I took him to the train station."

Miss Margot turned nearly as pale as her mannequin self. "You just abandoned the child? He could be anywhere."

"That's right," Double W said. "He could be anywhere."

"You wouldn't even know him if you saw him. He could have ended up in your soup pot."

"Anything is possible," Double W agreed.

Before Jackson could try to tell Miss Margot what had happened, she jerked her arm straight out and pointed a trembling finger. "This is your day of reckoning. Wanda Lovecraft, I cast a spell on you. *Caput lupinum.*" What Jackson heard was KAH-puut loo-PEE-nuum.

Double W, looking surprised, sprouted furry ears and the grizzled snout of what – a fox? A coyote? Then she laughed. "*Wear the wolf's head*? Is that the best you can do?" She muttered a few words and shook out her curls as her head returned to normal.

Her finger shaking even more, but still pointing, Miss Margot fired again: "Wanda Lovecraft, I cast a spell on you. *In aqua scribis.*" Double W walked over to the kettle and started swirling a finger in the soup.

"What are you doing?" Jackson yelled. "Finish her off."

"I'm trying," Miss Margot said. "I don't know that much Latin."

"Forget the Latin," Leon urged.

"But the ancient language is more powerful," Miss Margot said. "See."

It was true that Double W seemed to be weaker, and struggling to stop her finger from writing in the soup water. Again, though, she muttered a few words and seemed to return to herself. "Enough of this nonsense," she said and pointed her own finger at Miss Margot. "Margo, I cast a spell on *you*." Miss Margot slumped to the floor.

173

"Wow," Alonzo said. Jackson could have kicked Alonzo for the admiration in his voice. "If you two can do all that, how come you don't just turn twigs and stuff into whatever you want?"

"The more magic energy they use, the more it uses them up," Indira observed.

Double W turned a displeased eye to the group. "You think you can outwit me," she said. She walked – a little unsteadily, Jackson thought – over to Truly and grabbed her by the scruff of her neck. "Another ingredient for my soup."

"No," Indira said. "I've got your elixir." She slipped a bottle of dark liquid from her backpack.

"More trickery," Double W said, holding Truly over the pot.

"Drop the cat, I drop the bottle," Indira said. "And you look like you need it. Your complexion is all pasty and your eyelids are drooping."

"More deceit," Double W said, but she hesitated. "One of you drink first. If it's toxic to you, it may benefit me."

Indira unstoppered the bottle.

"Are you nuts?" Leon asked.

"I'll just take a sip," Indira said. "A little shouldn't do anything more to me than make me throw up."

"You don't know that," Leon said. "You might poison yourself."

Jackson grabbed the bottle from her. "I'll do it." He was the one that had gotten all of them into this mess. He brought the bottle to his lips and let the liquid trickle into his mouth.

174

It was the foulest, most bitter taste he could imagine. He held the bottle out to Double W. She took the vessel from him. "Swallow," she said.

Jackson pretended to gulp. He grabbed his stomach.

Double W smiled. "Finally, the real elixir of longevity." She dropped Truly, tipping the bottle and drinking deeply from it. Immediately, she tried to spit it out, just as Jackson was doing. "Elderberry!" she cried. "Echinacea!"

It was too late. She burst into a shower of particles that sent Truly limping for the front door. Evelyn trotted over to examine the remaining dark stone, sniffing and tentatively batting at it. Satisfied, he ran to the door and escaped. Miss Margot roused herself and regarded the black heart. She tried to rise, but failed. "*Abest,*" she whispered. The heart disappeared. So did Miss Margot. Vanished. *Absent.*

"Wow," Alonzo said. "She spelled herself."

Jackson picked up Truly, who was shivering by the door. "It's over," he said. "Let's go."

Once again they stood on the sidewalk outside 42 Crab Apple St. "Do you think they're really gone?" Alonzo asked.

"I don't think you can come back from a spell like that," Jackson said. Jackson would never know what Miss Margot could tell him about his family.

"If we're done battling evil, I need to get home for supper," Leon said. "Mom's picking up burgers from the diner."

"How can you eat meat after Wanda Lovecraft accused us of being as wicked as her?" Indira asked.

Leon raised his hands in the air and pretended to take a big bite. "Like this," he said.

"That was pretty good," Alonzo said. "Maybe I could use you in my show."

"What show?" Jackson asked, stroking Truly's fur.

"I'm writing a script about a little town suddenly struck by a dark force," he said.

"You are?" Indira asked.

"I'm about to," Alonzo said. "Maybe you could be my offstage narrator."

"Why can't I be onstage?" Indira demanded.

Jackson waved a hand and walked away, leaving his friends to debate about roles and scenes. Friends. Before all this started, he hadn't really known those kids. Now he had friends brave enough – or, he thought with a smile, dumb enough – to stick by him.

All his troubles hadn't vanished like Double W. Rodney would still be a problem. Grandpa might get worse. He still had to figure out what to do about Mr. Dewey.

But he'd learned that he could think on his own when he had to, and he'd learned that he could call upon friends when he needed them. A little furry head bumping him under the chin reminded him that he didn't have to feel alone any more.

Jackson hurried home. He found himself actually hoping there'd be buckwheat noodles on the table. But after supper, he intended to magic that Halloween candy out of his parents.

Justice

The wind and the huge gray cloud returned to Glasglen to find a boy hurrying home, carrying a little cat. Three arguing children paused to look up at the sudden darkening of the sky.

Wind and Cloud glided along Crab Apple Street, stopping to linger at number 42. Wind howled. Cloud glowered. When they received no answer, Cloud began to lighten, revealing a happy, rosy twilight hue.

Wind urged Cloud to sweep on to Railroad Avenue, past the depot and the police station. A fluffy white cat grooming itself on the stoop outside the police station looked up and scowled at Cloud. Wind laughed and blew a kiss, leaving the cat's just-licked coat standing in spiky tufts.

Wind sneezed, shaking the leaves from the oaks stubbornly clinging to their browning foliage. Cloud followed Wind as it blew past the funeral home and behind Dewey's Department Store, where they found the back door propped open as a man struggled to move a mangled machine out of the store.

Delighted by the discovery of an open door, Wind swooped inside, swirling and twirling like a ballerina, then huffing and puffing like a fairy tale wolf. Merchandise blew through the door and out into the town. The naked oaks found themselves draped in bright silk scarves, white handkerchiefs and black socks.

Wind danced around the display suitcase, which began rolling like a tumbleweed, rattling through the door before hitting a bump outside. The latch collapsed, the suitcase fell open and bills soared through the air.

The man jigged like Rumpelstiltskin, leaping and trying to grab at the money. The pieces of paper floated beyond his reach, flying off to plaster the distant hillside with splatterings of green.

Cloud laughed and laughed, its rosy hue darkening to purple, and suddenly the man found himself standing in rain, shaking his head at the sight of his soggy merchandise and the sound of the drops pinging on his ruined press. The rain-drenched bills fell from the trees, disintegrating into pulpy puddles.

A long, loud whistle interrupted Wind and Cloud's play. They paused to watch the lights flashing at the railroad crossing. Just for fun, Wind and Cloud chased the train, following the convoy of cars out of town.

End

Acknowledgments

I want to thank my first readers – Julie Weston, Gina Vitolo, Sarah Rubush and my editor extraordinaire, Cat Pleska. Thanks, also, to my first listeners, including the students at the Ruffner Elementary assembly arranged by Paul Epstein. Thank you, Jeanne Brenneman and Eric Fritzius, for bringing your talents to the cover.

I appreciate the information provided by audiologist L. Ashley Epling, of Greenbrier Audiology and Hearing Aid Services, Inc. The Latin phrases came from *Veni, Vidi, Vici: Conquer Your Enemies, Impress Your Friends with Everyday Latin*, by Eugene Ehrlich.

Alderson's Store was the inspiration for the setting of Dewey's Department Store. But while Miss Margot was a permanent fixture in Mr. Dewey's store, Betty Alderson's displays are ever changing and always charming. Alderson, West Virginia, with its historic train depot and other notable architecture, also provided setting inspiration. I even used some of the street names, because I liked them so much. It's a great town. (Alderson is not in a National Radio Quiet Zone, but as of this writing, there really is one in West Virginia at the National Radio Astronomy Observatory in Green Bank.)

Thank you to Mountain State Press, a literary nonprofit press dedicated to publishing the varied voices of West Virginia. Thanks to board President Bill Haydon, for his many years of dedication, and to Rhonda Castle for her unwavering, and valuable, assistance. Thanks also to board member Gil Brooks.

And to all my family and friends – thank you for your support.

About the Author

If you're looking for Belinda Anderson, you might find her:

- Perusing the kids' section of any library. She tells the library staff she's checking out the books for research, but really, she loves reading them for herself, especially books with fantastical plots and settings.

- Visiting schools and organizations as an author. We won't mention the time she kept circling a school, trying to find the right entrance door. It was a big school!

- Teaching creative writing workshops at schools, libraries and conferences. We also won't mention the time she was pressing down so hard while writing on a chalkboard that the chalk broke, with one sizeable piece ricocheting off her forehead and dropping neatly into her blouse pocket.

- Strolling around town or hiking a nature trail. She gets some of her best ideas while walking.

Belinda's literary work was selected for inclusion on the first official literary map of West Virginia, published by Fairmont State University. Belinda's fiction also has received national recognition, including awards for several of the short stories first collected in the

The Well Ain't Dry Yet, now in its second printing by Mountain State Press. Read the chapter that introduced Twilight Dawn at the author's web site: www.BelindaAnderson.com. Mountain State Press also published her most recent collections, *The Bingo Cheaters* and *Buckle Up, Buttercup.*

Belinda also has been named a Master Artist by the West Virginia Division of Culture and History, working with emerging writers as a mentor through a grant program.

"We are enriched by the creative acts of reading and writing," she says. "Reading engages our imagination and writing gives us the opportunity to connect with one another."

41562202R00117

Made in the USA
Charleston, SC
01 May 2015